Anthologies

CRAVINGS
(with Laurell K. Hamilton, Rebecca York, Eileen Wilks)

BITE
(with Laurell K. Hamilton, Charlaine Harris, Angela Knight, Vickie Taylor)

KICK ASS
(with Maggie Shayne, Angela Knight, Jacey Ford)

MEN AT WORK
(with Janelle Denison, Nina Bangs)

DEAD AND LOVING IT
SURF'S UP
(with Janelle Denison, Nina Bangs)

MYSTERIA
(with P. C. Cast, Gena Showalter, Susan Grant)

OVER THE MOON
(with Angela Knight, Virginia Kantra, Sunny)

DEMON'S DELIGHT
(with Emma Holly, Vickie Taylor, Catherine Spangler)

DEAD OVER HEELS
MYSTERIA LANE
(with P. C. Cast, Gena Showalter, Susan Grant)

"What can you say about a vampire whose loyalty can be bought by designer shoes? Can we say, outrageous?"
—*The Best Reviews*

Undead and Unfinished

"An entertaining read and the most complex of the series."
—*Monsters and Critics*

"[Davidson] proves she can skillfully combine creepy and chilling with numerous laugh-out-loud moments."   —*Bitten by Books*

Undead and Unwelcome

"Pads a chic coffin."   —*The Denver Post*

"Outrageously wacky."   —*RT Book Reviews*

Undead and Unworthy

"One that fans don't dare miss."   —*Darque Reviews*

"I can't wait to see what happens next. All hail Queen Betsy!"
—*Night Owl Reviews*

Undead and Uneasy

"Be prepared to fall in love with the Undead all over again!"
—*Romance Reviews Today*

"When it comes to outlandish humor, Davidson reigns supreme!"
—*RT Book Reviews*

"Ms. Davidson has her own brand of wit and shocking surprises that make her vampire series one of a kind."
—*Darque Reviews*

continued . . .

UNDEAD *AND* UNDERMINED

MaryJanice Davidson

JOVE BOOKS, NEW YORK

THE BERKLEY PUBLISHING GROUP
Published by the Penguin Group
Penguin Group (USA) Inc.
375 Hudson Street, New York, New York 10014, USA

Penguin Group (Canada), 90 Eglinton Avenue East, Suite 700, Toronto, Ontario M4P 2Y3, Canada
(a division of Pearson Penguin Canada Inc.) • Penguin Books Ltd., 80 Strand, London WC2R 0RL,
England • Penguin Group Ireland, 25 St. Stephen's Green, Dublin 2, Ireland (a division of Penguin
Books Ltd.) • Penguin Group (Australia), 250 Camberwell Road, Camberwell, Victoria 3124, Australia
(a division of Pearson Australia Group Pty. Ltd.) • Penguin Books India Pvt. Ltd., 11 Community
Centre, Panchsheel Park, New Delhi—110 017, India • Penguin Group (NZ), 67 Apollo Drive,
Rosedale, Auckland 0632, New Zealand (a division of Pearson New Zealand Ltd.) • Penguin Books
(South Africa) (Pty.) Ltd., 24 Sturdee Avenue, Rosebank, Johannesburg 2196, South Africa

Penguin Books Ltd., Registered Offices: 80 Strand, London WC2R 0RL, England

This is a work of fiction. Names, characters, places, and incidents either are the product of the author's
imagination or are used fictitiously, and any resemblance to actual persons, living or dead, business
establishments, events, or locales is entirely coincidental. The publisher does not have control over
and does not have any responsibility for author or third-party websites or their content.

UNDEAD AND UNDERMINED

A Jove Book / published by arrangement with the author

PUBLISHING HISTORY
Berkley Sensation hardcover edition / July 2011
Jove mass-market edition / May 2012

Copyright © 2011 by MaryJanice Alongi.
Excerpt from *Undead and Unstable* copyright © 2012 by MaryJanice Alongi.
Cover art by Don Sipley.
Cover design by Lesley Worrell.
Text design by Kristin del Rosario.

ISBN: 978-0-515-15091-9

JOVE®
Jove Books are published by The Berkley Publishing Group,
a division of Penguin Group (USA) Inc.,
375 Hudson Street, New York, New York 10014.
JOVE® is a registered trademark of Penguin Group (USA) Inc.
The "J" design is a trademark of Penguin Group (USA) Inc.

PRINTED IN THE UNITED STATES OF AMERICA

10 9 8 7 6 5 4 3 2 1

ALWAYS LEARNING   **PEARSON**

To all the readers
who assumed I'd lost my teeny,
tiny mind after Unfinished,
but hung in anyway, my deepest thanks.

Acknowledgments

Where, oh where to begin? For starters, book ten? Book *ten?* Holy Fritos, Batman. Even as I typed that I felt my jaw sag. Book ten? How'd that happen? Am I proud? Am I freaked? Am I taking a bow? Am I talking to myself, and more important, can I stop? Or am I just ducking away from a well-deserved smack?

So, ten books! Weird. This is proof that goofing off in high school and not going to college were excellent decisions on my part. Who's laughing now, Honor Society? Huh?

Anyway, thanks for reading 'em.

Thanks also to my terrific assistant, Tracy "You Don't Scare Me" Fritze. She knows exactly what she's getting into (for two years now!), yet she keeps coming back. It's baffling to me.

My folks, for telling strangers about my books and urging people they've never met to buy them. My sister, who travels almost as much as I do, because she always

Acknowledgments

calls me from whichever airport bookstore she's seen my books in. "Add DC to the list!" she'll chortle into my voice mail, "and you still haven't given back my cake pan." Yeah, well, you can choke waiting for that cake pan. It's awesome and I'm not giving it up.

My dear friends Cathie Carr and Stacy Sarette, who are remarkably patient with me when I disappear off their radar for months at a time. I don't deserve them, but at least I know it.

Special thanks to my friend Austin Robinson-Coolidge, who told me a decade ago when the tea craze was starting that, to him, chai tasted like Glade air freshener. I finally got around to stealing that and making Betsy think it. Ha! Ponder *that* next time you're staggering your way through a marathon, ARC.

And finally, my in-laws and husband, who had a shitty year but never flinched. I'm always amazed by their core strength. It's like their bones are lined with titanium or something. Oooh! Like Wolverine, except not tortured and angry and berserk-ey. Usually.

"My God, your mother-in-law beat a burglar to death with her walker!" "Yeah, she doesn't like people touching her things." My in-laws are like superheroes, except people are scared shitless of them.

—MaryJanice, Winter 2010

Author's Note

The most luxurious RV in the world, which Betsy calls the Mansion on Wheels, and which Jessica refers to as the Mystery Machine, really exists! I didn't make any of that up. I don't know if that's cool or weird.

Also, I've never been to the Cook County Morgue, but I'm sure it's very nice. And unfortunately, bodies have gone missing there in the past. But I'm sure they've got that all worked out by now.

Finally, this book is essentially a trilogy within a series, and *Undermined* is the second book. *Undead and Unstable* will follow. So if you finish this book and find you still have questions, there'll be another Betsy book coming down the pike in about twelve months or so.

The Story So Far

Betsy "Please Don't Call Me Elizabeth" Taylor was run over by a Pontiac Aztek about three years ago. She woke up the queen of the vampires and in dazzling succession (but no real order), bit her friend Detective Nick Berry, moved from a Minnesota suburb to a mansion in St. Paul, solved various murders, attended the funerals of her father and stepmother, became her half brother's guardian, avoided the room housing the Book of the Dead (*Book of the Dead*, noun, the vampire bible written by an insane vampire on flesh, which causes madness if read too long in one sitting), cured her best friend's cancer, visited her alcoholic grandfather (twice), solved a number of kidnappings, realized her husband/king, Eric Sinclair, could read her thoughts (she could always read his), and found out the Fiends had been up to no good (*Fiend*, noun, a vampire given only animal [dead] blood, a vampire who quickly goes feral).

Also, her roommate Antonia, a werewolf from Cape Cod, took a bullet in the brain for Betsy, saving her life. The stories about bullets not hurting vampires are not true; plug enough lead into brain matter and that particular denizen of the undead will never get up again. Garrett, Antonia's lover, killed himself the instant he realized she was dead forever.

As if this wasn't enough of a buzzkill, Betsy soon found herself summoned to Cape Cod, Massachusetts, where Antonia's Pack leaders lived. Though they were indifferent to the caustic werewolf in life, now that she was dead in service to a vampire, several thousand pissed-off werewolves had a few questions. ("What, now? You care, *now*?")

While Betsy, Sinclair, BabyJon, and Jessica were on the Cape answering well-it's-a-little-late-*now* questions, Marc, Laura, and Tina remained in Minnesota (Tina to help run things while her monarchs were away, Marc because he couldn't get the vacation time, and Laura because she was quietly cracking up).

They hadn't been gone long before Tina disappeared and Marc noticed devil worshippers kept showing up in praise of Laura, the Antichrist.

In a muddled, misguided attempt to help (possibly brought on by the stress of his piss-poor love life—as an ER doc, Marc worked hours that would make a unionless sweatshop manager cringe), he suggested to Laura that she put her "minions" to work helping in soup kitchens and such.

As sometimes happens, Laura embraced the suggestion with zeal. Then she took it even further, eventually deciding her deluded worshippers could help get rid of all sorts of bad elements . . . loan officers, bail jumpers, contractors who overcharge, and . . . vampires.

Meanwhile, on the Cape, Betsy spent time fencing with Michael Wyndham, the Pack leader responsible for three hundred thousand werewolves worldwide, and babysitting Lara Wyndham, future Pack leader and current first grader.

With Sinclair's help (and Jessica's cheerful-yet-grudging babysitting of BabyJon), Betsy eventually convinced the werewolves she meant Antonia no harm, that she in fact liked and respected the woman, that she was sorry Antonia was dead and would try to help Michael in the future . . . not exactly a debt, more an acknowledgment that because she valued Antonia and mourned her loss, she stood ready to assist Antonia's Pack.

Also, Betsy discovered her half brother/ward was impervious to paranormal or magical interference. This was revealed when a juvenile werewolf Changed for the first time and attacked the baby, who found the entire experience amusing, after which he spit up milk and took a nap.

Though the infant could be hurt, he could *not* be hurt by a werewolf's bite, a vampire's sarcasm, a witch's spell, a fairy's curse, a leprechaun's dandruff . . . like that. Betsy was amazed—she suspected there was something off about the baby, but had no idea what it could be. ("I was thinking . . . bred-in-the-bone Republican. Just really, really evil.")

Sinclair, who until now had merely tolerated the infant, instantly became besotted ("That's *my* son, you know.") and began plotting—uh, thinking—about the child's education and other necessities.

Back at the ranch (technically the mansion on Summit Avenue in St. Paul), Laura had more or less cracked up. She had fixed it so Marc couldn't call for help (when he discovered their cells no longer worked, he snuck off to find another line, only to be relentlessly followed by devil worshippers who politely but firmly prevented this), and she and her followers were hunting vampires.

Betsy finally realized something was wrong (via a badly garbled text secretly sent by a hysterical Marc), and they returned to the mansion in time to be in the middle of a Vampires vs. Satanists Smackdown.

Betsy won, but only because Laura pulled the killing blow at the last moment.

People went their separate ways, for a while. And nobody felt like talking.

Three months later, Betsy decided to take the Antichrist by the, uh, horns, and invited her to go shoe shopping at the Mall of America. It was at this time she learned the Antichrist was fluent in every language on earth and had little or no working knowledge of big-screen devils. Thus, Betsy hauled her sis home for a devil-a-thon (including Al Pacino's Satan, Elizabeth Hurley's sexy devil, the baby in *Rosemary's Baby*, and Damien Thorn in *The Omen*). It was at this time Laura confessed that she feels guilty whenever she's interested in finding out more about herself, her capabilities, or her mom, Satan. ("It's like I'm slapping my adopted mom and dad in the face by wondering about her.") It's also at this time that Betsy realized she was sick of having a never-fail resource in her own home, the Book of the Dead, which she doesn't dare use because anyone who reads it for longer than twenty minutes or so goes insane.

So she and Satan struck a deal, which actually made sense at the time: Betsy would help Laura embrace and use her supernatural powers, and in return the devil would fix it so Betsy could read the book without the accompanying nut-jobbery.

In addition to Laura's weapons (stabbing weapons or a crossbow, which normally stay in hell unless she calls them up), she learned she can teleport almost anywhere. Cool, right? Yeah, not so much. In fact, that turned out to be a huge problem, as any*where* encompasses any*when*. In rapid, annoying succession, Betsy and Laura found themselves in Salem, Massachusetts, during the witch hunts of the 1600s; Hastings, Minnesota, before the spiral bridge was replaced (so, anywhere between 1895 and 1951); and the future.

A thousand years in the future. Also, the future? Sucks. There was some sort of cataclysmic global thingummy and Minnesota in the future has winters even worse than the ones it has now. Nobody wants to worry about heat exhaustion on the Fourth of July, but frostbite and hypothermia are just as bad . . . and since the average temperature in July 3015 is thirty below, nobody's getting rich off selling sunscreen.

In fact, nobody—except Future Betsy—is getting rich, period. They're mostly hanging out in belowground enclaves and focusing on not dying.

To make matters even yuckier, Future Marc is a vampire. And not just any vampire . . . after hundreds of years of being Betsy's personal whipping vampire, he's dangerously insane. So much so that Laura and Betsy can feel how *wrong* he is after a glance. In fact, neither of them can bear to look him in the eyes, or even be around him.

BabyJon was there, too, and he's as charismatic and charming as Marc is creepy and nutso. He wouldn't tell Betsy how he could be walking around one thousand years in the future and not be a vampire, though she tried and tried to wheedle it out of him.

In the forty-five minutes or so they were in the future, they discovered Future Betsy had taken over (most of) the country, could raise and control zombies, and had a crippling lack of empathy for anyone. More troubling, Sinclair and Tina were *nowhere* to be found. Worse, no one would even talk about them . . . except Undead Marc, until Ancient Betsy shut him up and sent him away. And BabyJon was wildly uncomfortable about the subject.

They returned, vowing to figure out a way to save the future. Or undo it. Laura teleported Betsy back to the mansion and went on her merry, hell-bound way.

Betsy returned to find out Tina and Sinclair remember meeting her in the past. They explained that they'd always known Betsy would be headed on a time-travel romp, and the only way to help her was to stay out of the way.

To Betsy's amazement, Jessica is heavily pregnant (wedding ring?) by Nick Berry. And Nick is happy to see her . . . since Betsy prevented her younger self from feeding on him, he didn't experience any vamp trauma this time around, so now they're very close friends.

Now Betsy has to explain to her loved ones about the future, about the fact that they're living in a tampered timeline, and figure out a way to, as Betsy would put it, "Get bad shit done."

Dishonesty is a thief of time, of energy, of pride. We must remember—and teach our children (and perhaps our political figures)—one essential: the truth shall make you free.

—MARTHA STEWART

Undermine (un*der*mine): 1) to excavate the earth beneath; 2) to wash away supporting material from; 3) to subvert or weaken insidiously or secretly; 4) to weaken or ruin by degrees.

—*MERRIAM-WEBSTER*

Yeah, they're undermining me. Not digging underneath me. The other thing. The weakening me behind my back thing. It just sucks.

—BETSY TAYLOR, QUEEN OF THE VAMPIRES

Paranoid? Well, that just confirms all my suspicions!

—JENNA MARONEY, *30 ROCK*

Retroactive Continuity: Refers to the deliberate alteration of previously established facts in a work of serial fiction. Retcons may be carried out for a variety of reasons, such as to accommodate sequels or further derivative works in the same series, to reintroduce popular characters, to resolve chronological issues, to reboot a familiar series for modern audiences, or to simplify an excessively complex continuity structure.

—WIKIPEDIA, OCTOBER 4, 2011

Undead and Undermined

When the awful racket started up, when the coroner got
ready to open my skull with what I later found out was a
Stryker autopsy saw, I was fine with it.

No, more than that . . . it seemed like a really, really good
idea. Not just a good idea for me. It would be great for
everyone involved. And if you took the long view, it would
be good for humanity. Because I'd had enough. Case closed,
everybody out of the pool, time to shut off the lights and
lock up, hit the trail, shake a leg, beat feet, get gone, get out.

I was out.

How sucky was it that I knew, *knew* the one thing worse
than waking up on an embalming table was waking up

inside a body bag? I did not ever want to know that. *No one should know that.*

Oh, and while we're compiling a list of things no one should know? No one should know that they grow up—grow old, anyway—to torture their friends. That they either brought about (or didn't bother to prevent) a scary-ass nuclear winter apocalyptic event resulting in the very real possibility of freezing to death on the Fourth of July.

No one should know that, on the off chance they turn into an ancient evil vampire crone, they forget all sense of fun and, worse, fashion. Gray dresses! What the *fuck*?

So even though the buzzing whine of the saw felt like the coroner was *already* slicing me open, I laid still and did my impersonation of a corpse.

Hey, everybody's good at something.

Graham Benson lit a cigarette with trembling fingers. He did not smoke but had been able to score a butt and a lighter from a member of the I'm-Cutting-Back-I-Swear tribe. Graham did not smoke, had never smoked, but was determined to start immediately.

The door to the doctor's lounge wheezed open and Graham observed his attending, the extraordinarily hairy Dr. Carter (and didn't the two of them get shit, Dr. Benson and

Dr. Carter? Like he needed another reason to hate NBC), practically tiptoe into the close, windowless, burnt-coffee-and-disinfectant-smelling room.

Carter's beard had recently been trimmed, so the ends merely brushed his throat instead of his nipples. His dark, curly chest hair was trying to burst through his scrubs shirt. He had begged permission to jettison the de rigueur lab coat and, after he'd proven to the other chief residents that his mat of body hair kept him adequately warm, they relented. Hairy Carter was perturbing enough; Sweaty Red-faced Hairy Carter was an abomination unto the Lord.

"Sooooo." Carter coughed. It sounded like a truck laboring uphill in the wrong gear. "Bad night, Dr. Benson?"

"It's the wee hours of the morning, Carey." This was a breach of etiquette; interns and residents did not call department heads by their first names without invitation. And Graham would never, ever ask. Nor would he ever think twice about breaking any etiquette guideline. His intelligence, drive, and skill were why he got away with it.

"'Bad night' isn't just dumb, Carey. And it isn't just inaccurate. It's dumb. And, yeah. I said that already." He sucked on the sullenly smoldering cigarette and thought, *Millions of people smoke these things? Several times a day? For years? Voluntarily? I was right all along: 99.5% of the human race is comprised by idiots, and the other 0.5% by morons.*

"Listen, we're all with you. Except for your new weird habit. I'm worried about you." Benson shook his head at the almost-extinguished cigarette. "And there's not a person in this department who doesn't sympathize."

He fingered his collar. The scrubs were soft from many washings. "Lie."

"There's at least one person in this department who sympathizes, probably."

"Gee whiz. I feel so much better. The steaming, fretful masses view me with pity. Or at least one does. Probably."

"You have to admit, it's not every day a patient wakes up in the middle of an—"

Graham felt his teeth meet, and most of the cigarette fell out of his mouth, decapitated by his involuntarily chomp. "She didn't wake up, she was *dead*. She wasn't in a coma. She didn't have hypothermia. *She was dead*. There was nothing to wake up *from*."

"Okay, Graham, but semantics won't—"

"Flatline! Brain dead! Pupils fixed and dilated! Body temp falling . . . body temp almost *room* temp, do you get that? Guess what? People don't wake up from that! You want to guess why? Because when you're at room temp, you! Are! *Dead!*" He grabbed at his neck again, restlessly kneading the fabric.

"So, help me out here, are you saying she woke up then yelled, or yelled and then woke up?"

Graham slumped forward and rested his forehead on the cracked, pitted tabletop. "You've come here to kill me, haven't you? But you've gotta bug me to death to do it, right? Remember your oath, doctor, and summon the decency to make it quick."

Finally! This must be the slowest or sleepiest coroner in the history of forensic science. It was like he didn't know there were people in his morgue who had an agenda. I couldn't speak for the other dead guys in this chilly tomb, but *I* couldn't afford to loll around on an autopsy table all night. I wondered if he knew how selfish he was being. Just because I was dead didn't mean I wasn't in a hurry.

Bad enough I had given up on life/death and was resigned to permanent exile to . . . where do the souls of sadistic despots-in-training go after death-for-real? Hell?

Not for what they've done, but what they *will* do? Or do we still get to heaven because we didn't live long enough to bring about (or don't bother to prevent) the end of the world? Because we hadn't quite gotten the chance to turn on friends and family in order to save our own ass?

Wherever I was supposed to end up, I'd be there in a couple more minutes. Then this would be done. I'd be done.

(Oh where oh Elizabeth where oh my own where are you?)

I softly groaned, which was drowned out by the saw. I could shut my eyes (as I was) and I could clamp my hands over my ears (which I didn't dare), but couldn't shut my brain off. Couldn't block my husband's thoughts.

I had to, though. His life and my soul depended on it.

"Of course I remember everything." Graham pinched the bridge of his nose. He wore the expression of a man forced to tolerate exceptional stupidity. He looked like that a lot. "It was half an hour ago. I'm freaked out, not brain dead."

"Do you . . . do you mind going over it again?"

"Of course I mind, you hirsute moron."

"You start a lot of sentences with 'of course.'"

"I get asked a lot of dumbass questions, of course. Did you catch how I mixed it up that time? And to answer your silly-ass question, I should be focusing on psychologically blocking the last hour, but I'm sitting here, aren't I? I haven't even gotten to the weirdest part yet, you believe that?"

His chief gave him a manly clap on the shoulder. The pathologist winced and prayed his shoulder hadn't been dislocated. "I want you to know we all get why you decided to work with dead people. No one ever thought that was anything but a spectacular idea. I say again: spectacular! We're just worried you're going to be hauled away in screaming hysterics and come back determined to do a peds rotation."

"Pediatrics?" Fresh horror swept over him like a freezing bath. "Never! I will never stock suckers! And I will never give out stickers! I will never say, 'My, how big you've grown!'"

"You're getting shrill again, Graham."

He resisted the urge to bang his head on the table. "I hate everyone. But you most of all."

"And the world continues to turn," his boss said with maddening cheer. "Soooo . . . you're still gung ho for the pathology residency?"

"What are the odds of another patient coming to life under my knife?" Cripes, his neck itched. "Look: I want the rest of the day off. I want you to deal with Admin and then I want you to go away. When I finish eating this cigarette, I'm outta here. I'll be back tomorrow by shift change. There's nothing else to talk about."

"How goes the psychological blocking?"

"It goes shitty. I can remember everything. Everything that happened and everything she said."

"So she did talk to you. Y'know, that's the weirdest of all. That she could be lucid after—"

"After what, coming back to life? Why wouldn't she be?

7

You're not listening, Chief: she was dead. Not in a coma. Dead. I'm concerned, Benson. You don't seem to be getting this."

"I'm concerned, too," said his boss—who really was an okay guy once you got used to his perpetually sunny mood— "but for different reasons."

"Weirdest night of my life, and I'm not a rookie, right? I've seen things; every path resident has. Shit, every *doctor* has. But the things she said, and then what she did, that was the weirdest of all, and I don't say that lightly."

"Far as I know, you've never said anything lightly."

"Including right now. She was completely dead one minute. And completely alive the next. What if—what if she had woken up when I cracked her sternum?" He could actually feel his mind trying to shy away from the image, distracting him by focusing on the woman's extraordinary good looks and charisma.

"She didn't, though." Benson coughed and shuffled his feet. He wasn't used to Graham wanting reassurance. And Graham wasn't used to needing it. "Everything's fine."

"This is *my* blood," he said quietly, touching the dark fabric. Path scrubs were dark brown, a superb choice for obvious reasons. His chief had made a natural assumption: the blood on his shirt was from the autopsy.

It was also an incorrect assumption.

"She bit me." He stared at the table. His irritation and panic and fright were subsiding into pissed off and horny. "She said she was sorry, after."

"She did *what*?"

"This is going to take much longer if you keep with all the dumb questions. Or did you need to look into getting a hearing aid? Can you hear me? Do you need a sign-language interpreter? Helloooooo?"

"You never mind my possible need for a hearing aid *or* sign language." Carter visibly relaxed. The irascible, touchy Graham was a known quantity. Not like the Graham of the last five minutes. "Tell the rest!"

So he did.

Don't answer him! And don't think.

Yeah, right. I could stop myself from telepathically answering the vampire king (who was the only person in existence with a telepathic ticket into my head, poor guy), but stop thinking about him? Suuure. Just like I could stop thinking about Manolo's new line or my near-continual thirst for blood.

Or the fact that, one day, I'll be a vicious, brittle tyrant more interested in raising zombies than saving my marriage . . . and my friends.

I didn't know how I'd gotten here. I didn't know what had happened to me. I had vague memories of some kind of argument . . . or was it an actual fight? Something about the devil . . . and my sister? Could that be right?

It probably wasn't right, dammit, and it didn't matter, either. I didn't know what had happened, and I was sticking with that story. And guess what? I didn't give a tin shit, either. My death was an excellent preventative for destroying the world.

(O my own Elizabeth where are you do not be hurt do not be hurt oh please please DO NOT BE HURT.)

I fought to keep my expression deadlike. I was an ordinary corpse in a room that was freezing. No shivering vampires here. Nobody sort of sentient on *this* table. (It had to be a table, something big and tall and made of steel . . . and freezing cold!)

If I let this happen to me, the world was safe. Better: Marc and Sinclair were safe.

Well. Safe from me, anyway. The king wouldn't be safe from all the vamps trying to fill the power vacuum once I was chopped up like a Cobb salad. But I couldn't think about that. I had to keep my focus; if I lived, the world was doomed. If I lived . . .

(WHERE ARE YOU? PLEASE PLEASE ANSWER, WHERE HAVE YOU GONE? WHO HAS TAKEN YOU?

ELIZABETH, FIGHT THEM, FIGHT THEM FIGHT THEM UNTIL I CAN FIGHT THEM FOR YOU!)

That was good advice, actually. Fight them until he could fight them for me. (He was so gloriously, stupidly chauvinistic at times.) Good advice . . . too bad I couldn't apply it to my situation. How could I fight myself? Especially when I was so evil and had such terrible taste in clothes, and was ancient and yucky?

Well. Let's think about that for a second. How could I? Maybe that was the wrong question; maybe I should be asking, how couldn't I? Who better to save him from me . . . than me? Would hiding and dying really be the best course of action? Or would it make things easier for the Big Bads meddling in our lives?

Or would it merely make things easier for me? God knew I tended to take the low road when it came to confrontation. The Antichrist and I had that in common. Was that it? Was I really that . . . that dimly lazy? Was this going to come about because I didn't want to do the work?

Tell you what: if I knew Sinclair was letting himself get killed to help me, I'd kick him in his undead 'nads. I'd scream at him until my eyes crossed. I'd dunk his big stupid head down a well. And kick him in his undead 'nads! And I'd be *right*.

Just like Sinclair was right.

I'd save him. I'd save us, I'd save the world. I had no idea how, and I had no idea what it would cost me. But I had to do it. Not because there was no one else, although there wasn't. Because it was my *job*. Or did I think the queen of the undead thing, as lame as it had always seemed to me, was something I could do part-time, like picking up extra shifts at McDonalds?

"She bit you?"

"Yeah. And it was the first thing that made sense that whole hour. Get it? She was a vampire. Those things are true. The stories are all true. Except . . ." He frowned, remembering.

"Oh, I can't wait to hear your 'except.' Hit me. Please not literally."

"Except, she wore a cross around her neck. A little gold one. But everything else fit. She really *was* dead when they brought her in, and when the sun went down. . . came back. And she asked where she was. I could tell she was trying to be nice. I could tell . . ."

Benson raised his eyebrows in silent encouragement. Graham had never seen the jolly path chief so wide-eyed.

"I could tell she was trying not to scare me."

"How did she do that? How did she seem?"

Graham grinned for the first time that evening. "Angry and naked. And smokin' hot." He groaned and rested his forehead on the table. "It's so wrong that I'm thinking about a vampire's awesome rack right now."

The buzzing whine of the saw was still filling the air . . . I'd had all these thoughts in about a second and a half. And it was getting louder, so the saw was getting closer.

Playtime was over. Should I or shouldn't I was over. Boohoo, I'm going to destroy the world so time to lie down and be dead was over, over, *over.*

I opened my eyes and caught the doc's wrist about a millimeter and a half from my hair. "You can't have my brain," I told the pale (and getting paler) fellow. "I need it to save my husband. And you, too, in a way."

I saw his thumb spasm and the whine of the saw lessened and then stopped altogether, tapering off with a sort of metallic moan: *BBBBZZZZZbbbbbzzzzbbbbzzzzzmmmm.* His mouth opened but nothing came out. Just as well, really. I wasn't interested in a lengthy conversation.

"I also need some clothes," I continued, sitting up and crossing my legs, and using my other arm to shield my tits. Which was stupid; he'd already seen me naked. In fact, I'd been nakedly exposed since he unzipped the body bag, then unceremoniously dumped me onto this big shiny table. *No* sheets! They just flop the naked corpses onto the tables where they can ogle our dead nudity, the pervs. *Law and Order* lied to me!

Oh, and the toe tag? Hurt like a *bitch*! (Who'd have thought? It hurts when someone ties a wire around your big toe and then cinches it tight. Savages.)

The poor doc dropped the big shiny saw-thingy, and I caught it before it could break half the bones of his foot. Far from being reassured by my swift, toe-saving action, he went whiter (if possible; could paper get paler? Could marshmallow fluff? Mmm, marshmallow fluff . . .) and backed away.

"Sorry to scare you."

Nothing.

"Uh, I don't suppose you know how I got here?"

Still nothing, this time accompanied by so much head shaking, at first I thought he was having a seizure.

I thought: *Better not get off the table and follow him across the room just yet. This was no time for the one who wasn't a corpse to get hysterical.*

I tried again. "Do you maybe know where I am? Come on, you must know where I am. Think hard. Hey, I'll even give you a hint: it's where *you* are. Anything? Bueller? Bueller? Also, stop staring at my tits."

"Dead," he told me.

"Betsy Taylor." I stuck out my hand. "I'll be the corpse you're not cutting up today. Maybe you should sit down." Worried, I hopped off the table and steadied him. "Listen, I'm not dangerous or anything." This was a gigantic lie, but one told in a good cause. The poor guy really did look like he was going to plant a header right in the middle of my freezing steel table.

"You didn't wake up," he explained, "you couldn't because you're *dead*." The doc was slender and short, with wispy blond hair and bulging blue eyes. His voice was a surprising baritone . . . I would have expected him to sound more reedy in his terror. "You didn't wake up. You couldn't wake up. Because you're dead."

"No, I didn't. And yep, I am. But while I was waiting for you to get down to it, I had a better idea then letting you chop up my brain, so I sprang into action, all heroic and determined to right wrongs and stuff. Wasn't it cool?"

I set down the saw. Ohhhh, boy. I was sooo thirsty. Poor guy. Feeding right now radically increased my chances of getting the hell out of here and back to the mansion. Thus, I would feed right now.

Poor guy.

"Listen, can I have some scrubs? Or my clothes? And maybe your car keys? And can I borrow your cell phone? Oh, hell, just give me everything you can get your hands on." I briskly clapped my hands in front of his face. "Dude! *Ándele.* That's Spanish for get your ass in gear, scrubs."

CHAPTER
ONE

SEVERAL HOURS EARLIER . . .

"Okay. I have to bring you up to speed. Okay? Sinclair?"

The king of the vampires was lying facedown on our bare mattress. Bare because in our doin'-it-like-monkeys frenzy, the sheets had been yanked and tattered, the pillows were in the bathtub, and at least two of the west windows were broken. The window guys downtown absolutely loved us. They've started giving us discounts.

"Hey! Are you listening?"

"Gummff ummf uhnn gunh." My husband was as loose and relaxed as I've ever seen him; I had marital-relationed him to death. (Almost.) He turned his head. "Allow me to enjoy the last of my postcoital coma, please."

"No time!"

"Why?" he mewled.

Note the date and time, please, and not because of all the time traveling. I didn't think Sinclair *could* mewl. Kittens did that. Whiny ex-wives. (Or whiny current wives.) Kids not getting their own way did that, grown women did that, and ouch, when they made that shrill extended meeeeeewwwllll, it felt like that icky earworm from *Wrath of Khan* drillin' in there.

Ech, I can hear Ricardo "Welcome to Fantasy Island" Montalban now from one of the least lame *Star Trek* movies: Their young enter through the ears and wrap themselves around the cerebral cortex; this has the yucky effect of rendering the poor things big-time susceptible to yucky suggestion and as they grow, yuckier and yuckier, madness and death are waiting for them in all their yuckiness, *gross*.

Anyway. I hate that noise and didn't think my husband could make it. But he could. The things I learn when I return from time travel and hell.

Huh. He was still talking.

"You are back, you are alive, you are beautiful and sated (at least I hope), you know all—"

"All? You think I know all? Clearly I came back in time and found the wrong Sink Lair. I'm trapped in a weird parallel universe where you still talk *all* the *time*." Seemed like

I spent half my afterlife waiting for him to take a breath so I could jump in. Also, vampires? Never need to take a breath. So you see what I've been dealing with.

"Phaugh, do not babble, due to your jaunts you know how we all came together in the recent past, because of the far past, and . . ." He trailed off. I waited. Knowing my husband, it'd be profound and life-changing. It'd help me see a disaster as a not-so-terrible disaster, probably. It'd convince me I wasn't alone in a cruel world. It'd . . . ". . . Mmzzzzz."

"Hey! Wake up!" I jabbed him in the bicep with my toe. Okay, I kicked him in the arm. He flopped bonelessly off the bed.

"I've missed your tender love play, Elizabeth," he groaned from the (ripped) carpet.

"We've got stuff to do!" I was looming over him without looking right at him, which is quite a trick. I didn't want to gaze into those dark, dark eyes, or eyeball his "day-amn, that's a nice ab-pack" or play follow-the-treasure-trail, or anything else that would lead to another forty-five minutes of bringing down the resale value of the entire wing.

"We've got things to explain!" I explained. Loudly. "So you need to focus. And also stop being naked. At least we don't have to deal with gross earworms from space—"

He blinked up at me. "Ah . . . what?"

"—but we've got other crap to wade through. Jessica wasn't pregnant when I left and I didn't know what a horse trough smelled like in Massachusetts and Minnesota. Whole planets have evolved between my ears!"

"*What?*" He sat up stiffly, like Frankenstein's monster, a big gorgeous well-hung Frankenstein with big black eyes that were wide with alarm.

"Exactly. Shit. To. Do. Are you on board now, Frank—uh, Sinclair? House meeting, stat! To the smoothie machine, Robin!" I darted off the bed, sheets trailing like a cape. I was Wonder Woman, I was Power Girl, I was—

Sinclairenstein reached out, flash-quick, and whipped the sheets away. It was like an evil, sexy magic trick. "Darling, is it your intention to show the household the color of your nipples? And that you have not one, but two dimples on your—"

"Shut up. I'll get dressed. Never mind my dimples."

"Oh, I never do," he said, surging to his feet so quickly, if I'd blinked I'd have missed it. "I don't mind this one—"

"Hey!"

"—or this one."

"*Yeeek!*"

CHAPTER
TWO

"You're probably all wondering why I've called you here." I tried, and failed, not to stare at Jessica's gigantic gut.

"Not really," The Thing with the Gut replied. "You're back from hell and chock-full of gossip."

"Intel," I grumbled. "Gossip is what old ladies do after church."

"Gossip is what *you* do, every day. And given the way you can't not stare at our kid," Nick added, sitting beside my best friend with an arm slung casually across her shoulders, "I'm guessing we're living in an altered time stream."

I gaped. I couldn't help it. Every word I had ever uttered since the age of twenty-nine months (shut up, I was a slow talker) ran right out of my brain. I was morbidly aware my mouth was hanging open, and prayed most of the bugs in the mansion were dead on one of a hundred windowsills and not flying around looking for something to fly into. "I, uh, well, that's a real time-saver for me. I'll come right out and admit it. I thought this would take longer to explain."

Wordlessly, they jerked their thumbs at Sinclair. Seeing me stare and flop still more, Jessica added, "You want the CliffsNotes version?"

"Are you two done? Sounds like you're done. Thank God you're done." Another roommate, Dr. Marc Spangler, shoved the swinging kitchen door open and marched straight to the blender, which was oozing with strawberry-banana smoothies. It was a lava flow of delicious strawberry-icy goodness!

He poured himself a generous cup, stared at the fridge where Tina kept her vodka, debated leaping off the wagon, decided to cling to said wagon for another hour, turned away from the fridge, and plopped onto one of the kitchen chairs around our big, wide wooden table. You could slaughter and dress a moose on the thing. We mostly just drank smoothies there, though.

A quick word about Tina's vodka collection. Like all vampires, she was constantly thirsty. Unlike many (*many* being my code for *less than a dozen*) she tried to keep it at bay with frozen drinks made from potatoes. She also adored variety. Not that you could tell from her schoolgirl-bait wardrobe.

Wait. Did schoolgirl-bait mean she was dressing to bait schoolgirls or was bait to people who liked—argh, focus!

Anyway, in our freezer lurked cinnamon-flavored vodka and bacon-flavored vodka. Ditto chili pepper and bison grass and bubble gum. Go ahead and barf . . . I nearly did.

"Now that you two've finished your unholy banging," Marc began, taking a monster slurp, "tell me all about the past. Is it smelly? Is the food great? Do they really say 'prithee'? And how come Laura's not here?"

"Laura didn't come back with me." Even as I said it I realized it was weird. "I mean, she made a doorway to here for me, but she stayed in hell. Or made herself a doorway and went to her apartment from hell. Or both. Or neither."

"Ah, beloved, one of the things I most cherish about you is your attention to detail."

"Yeah, well, I'll cherish you for shutting up now. I'm not my sister's keeper." Though if anyone needed one, the Antichrist qualified.

Marc was gulping his smoothie, and Jessica and Nick were watching him with some fascination. He had told me once that he'd gotten in the habit of bolting liquid meals when he was an intern. He could gulp down the equivalent of two pints of strawberries in three monster swallows. When he was off the wagon, he drank *all* his meals.

It was an indicator of how little I wanted to talk about

the future and the past by how interested I was letting myself get in something I was normally leery about discussing. "Uh, so, how are the AA meetings going?"

He cocked an eyebrow at me. "Don't take my inventory, Betsy."

"I don't know what that means," I admitted over Nick's snort.

"It means addicts in recovery know what they're supposed to do to stay clean and whether or not they're doing it. They dislike being reminded of it."

"Is that what you are?" Sinclair asked with interest. "In recovery?"

"Nah." Slurp. "People in recovery go to meetings. I'm a drunk."

I clapped a hand over my mouth, but not in time. Marc grinned at my insensitive titter.

I'd never understand why he couldn't find someone and settle down. He was smart, he was gorgeous, he had true green eyes (d'you know how rare that is? True green, not hazel?). He had black hair, currently cut brutally short into, I'm sorry to report, the Woody Harrelson. He was in his usual outfit of scrubs and his iPod. He was famous at the hospital for listening to heartbeats with one ear and They Might Be Giants in the other.

I know. They Might Be Giants? More like they might be one-hit wonders.

"But you know the old saying," Marc was saying, "tomorrow being another day and such. And I can't take credit for that . . . I think Stephen King said it first."

"Margaret Mitchell did."

"Not the another-day line. The addicts-go-to-AA line."

"Like you even read *Gone With the Wind*," I said. I mentioned how delighted I was in talking about stupid crap instead of the future, right? "Ha!"

Don't get me wrong. I didn't think there was much funny about addiction, outside of Sandra Bullock in *28 Days*. And I won't deny being mystified by *28 Days Later* . . . she was nowhere to be found in that one.

But Marc, so open about his sexuality, job, and love life, was weirdly closed about his drinking. There were times when he went to an AA meeting every day. And times when he didn't go for months. He'd made it clear ("Fuck off and die, again.") he appreciated zero interference, advice, or tough love.

Not that that would stop me! But I sort of had my hands full, what with an eternal nuclear winter-thing coming, my Ancient Evil Self, Jessica gestating The Thing That Made Her Eat Strawberry-banana Smoothies (she hated bananas), the Book of the Dead, and Satan doing her I'm-hot-and-plotting thing. But giving Marc unasked-for advice was on my to-do list, you bet. I was lulling him into a false sense of thinking he'd dodged nagging.

Yeah, I know. Even as I was telling myself this shit, I wasn't believing a word. Tell you what: if you can't fool yourself, you can't fool anybody.

I should cross-stitch that on a sampler.

"Did so," Nick replied. "Lost a bet."

"Huh? Oh, reading *Gone With the Wind*. And again, I say ha. Listen, Nick, if you'd even give the book a—"

"Stop that," he said with a shudder. "You know I hate that."

"Hate what?" The list was so long. Vampires . . . except apparently not anymore. Bananas . . . one of the few things he and Jess had in common. Bad guys . . . assuming he was still a cop. Tough to tell, because in the un-screwed timeline he'd been a plainclothes detective, so there was no uniform to give him away. But since he hung around cops and crime scenes and shooting ranges all day, he always smelled like gun powder; it was not an indicator of what his job was. In the altered timeline he could be in charge of sweeping up the men's room at the Cop Shop, or a gunsmith, for all I knew.

Luckily, he was still talking, because I badly needed enlightening. "Stop calling me Nick. You know I can't stand it."

I stared at him. For the second time in three minutes, I had no idea what to say. "What am I supposed to call you?"

"Maybe by his name?" Marc asked, pouring himself smoothie number three. Which was terrifying; I hadn't seen number two go down his gullet. I was starting to suspect sleeping with pretty boys and wolfing smoothies were his superpowers. "Just for funsies."

"Your name. Right. Right! Which is . . . ?" I prompted. "Sounds like . . . ?"

"Sounds like Dick."

"Hee, hee!"

"Grow up," Jessica and Nick (?) said in unison. Nick (?) added, "Come on, you *know* that. Or at least you knew it yesterday. Jeez, for the first year Jessica and I went out, you kept calling me by the wrong name."

"I do that to everyone. So your name is now Dick."

"It's always been Dick."

"But your name isn't Richard or Dick or anything like that. If you're a Nicholas, why would your nickname be Dick?"

"Because there are a lot of Nicks in my family, so they called me Dick to distinguish."

"Not Nick, yup, got it."

He sighed and looked put-upon, then smiled at me. "If only I could believe that, roomie."

Roomie! I sooo did not authorize this; it was annoying enough sharing hot water and fridge space with . . . uh . . .

lemmee see, how many people were living here before . . . "Are you still a cop?"

"No, now I sell Mary Kay." Seeing my eyes narrow into the cold pitiless gaze of a killer (or someone getting ripped at a sample sale), he elaborated: "Yes, I'm a cop. Currently Detective First Grade."

"And you . . . uh . . . you and Jessica . . ." I pointed vaguely at her big belly.

"Stop staring," she told me. "And yes. And stop that."

"I'm not staring."

"You absolutely are."

"I—oh, cripes, what was that?" I was on my feet before my brain knew I'd been trying to get away. "It moved!"

"Kicked," Jessica corrected, patting her belly and pushing the teeny foot or skull or tentacle out of the way. "But don't worry, honey. Someday you'll have hair on your special places and will start thinking about boys and wanting to have a baby."

"Fat fucking chance. No offense."

"Whoa, wait." Jessica's big brown eyes went squinty, which wasn't easy since she was wearing her hair skinned back in her usual eye-watering ponytail. She was sort of stuck in a high school hairdo, but it was understandable . . . pulling her hair back emphasized her cheekbones. You could practically cut yourself on them. She looked like a big round Nefertiti. "Did you just get back from hell and call me fat?"

"Not on purpose. Either of them."

"You're glowing, Jess, you're gorgeous," Nick soothed. "Betsy's just . . . you know. Being Betsy."

"What's that supposed to mean, Artist Formally Known as Nick?"

"What do you think it means, Vampire Queen Lamely Known as Betsy?" He sounded pissed, but then laughed. "Jesus! You take one trip to hell and then have to be reminded of the basics."

"Why are you laughing? You *hate* me!"

Nick frowned. "Since when?"

CHAPTER THREE

Well. Since I fed on him the night I came back from the dead,
and my husband mind-raped him. Oh, and since he forced
Jessica to choose between him and me. If we're, you know,
going to get down to specifics.

"Nicholas J. Berry!" Jessica gasped. "What is the matter with
you?"

"With me? You should have seen this psycho bitch in
action."

"That is enough," she snarled, hands on scrawny hips. "When
are you going to get it through your head that Betsy isn't the cause
of all your problems?"

I was frantically trying to signal to Jessica, making a slashing *motion across my throat, the universal gesture for* shush! *Although it made me sad, I felt Nick's rage was a perfectly appropriate reaction to the evening's festivities. I appreciated Jessica sticking up for me—she always stuck up for me—but she didn't have all the facts.*

He had been attacked. Again. Violated by vampires . . . again. I was amazed he hadn't gone fetal in the hedges.

"How many times do I have to say it," Jessica was saying. "How many times do you have to see it? She's a good guy!"

"No, Jess, it's okay, he—"

"She drinks blood, because she's dead," he said, spitting on the floor—spitting blood, I might add, and I was ashamed, because my fangs were out again. I didn't dare speak anymore; I didn't want him to know I wanted to drink and drink and drink. "She's a killer, and you know it."

"I love her, she's the sister I never got, and you know that."

"Ah, perhaps we could, ah, step into another room and discuss, ah, the new terms for surrender," Tina said, because even the Fiends looked uncomfortable to be witnessing the lovers' quarrel.

"Or maybe you could talk about this later, when everybody's calmed down," I tried.

"Don't make me choose," Jessica warned, ignoring us. For her, the only person in the room was Nick.

"I'm not making you choose. I'm choosing. We're done." He

wiped his face again, and we all pretended not to notice how his hand shook and how he couldn't look at her.

"That's right," Jessica replied coolly. "We are."

And just like that—it was over. They were over. We could all practically hear the snap.

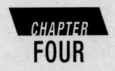

CHAPTER
FOUR

Except it wasn't. Because I'd never fed on Nick/Dick in this new reality. And for the first time, instead of being weirded out or scared by an out-of-the-blue change, I thought maybe that was a really good thing. How often in life do we get a do-over?

"Are you married? Was I there? What did I wear? Tell me you got married in the spring. Tell me I got to break out the Christian Louboutin Dahlia pointy toe ankle boots. It's almost too much to hope for!"

"It's awful that you're talking about the shoes, and everybody at this table knows you're talking about the shoes."

"It's not such a high heel, is the thing. I could have walked around in them no matter how long the ceremony was, without ever praying for anesthetic." I turned to Sinclair. "I can recover from bullet wounds but my feet still hurt after a couple of hours in pumps? The hell!"

Jessica frowned. "Wait. Who—?"

"We aren't married." Dick-Nick said. "Yet. But nice work making our non-marriage all about you, Bets."

Well, it is. I decided not to explain that out loud. *It really is! A little, anyway.* My Christian Louboutin ankle boots were the real victim here.

Jessica tried, and failed, to fold her arms over her titanic gut. "Don't even start with that 'not yet' crap."

"Yes," Sinclair hastily put in. "Don't."

"Oh, come on." Marc grinned. "Don't deprive me of drama. I need it! Like Jenna says, drama is my Gatorade; it replenishes my electrolytes."

Ah! Something else consistent in this universe: Marc was as devoted to Jenna Maroney's character from *30 Rock* as he was when I left. Weird, the things that made me feel better.

"And the reason the answer is 'not yet' instead of 'six months and going strong' is because your best friend," D-Nick was telling me, "has it in her head that because her mom and dad's marriage was a disaster, she, too, would be bad at it."

I could feel my eyes widen but didn't say anything. I thought Jess would make N/Dick a great wife. Hmm, gorgeous and smart and open-minded and cool and rich? Jessica should sink her claws into his hide and grip like an IRS agent looking for a promotion.

But her concerns were real. And I didn't think they should be brushed aside.

"Come on, don't be like that," Marc coaxed in an encouraging tone. "Look at the facts. If Betsy can be good at marriage, anyone can."

"Die screaming," I told him. Then snapped my jaw shut so quickly I almost bit off my tongue. I had the awful feeling that he did just that. Or would someday do just that. Goddamned time travel.

"I'm not having this discussion during smoothie time," Jessica told N/Dick.

"Indeed," Sinclair tried again, "there are other things we should—"

"That's it." D/Nick threw his arms in the air like a football referee ("And . . . it's gooooood!"). "I'm going to get Marc to dose you with tranqs, then haul you in front of a judge. By the time you—"

"Remember you've never been a fan of felony kidnapping or drug abuse," Marc prompted.

"—realize what's happened, it'll be too late. You'll be Mrs. Detective Nicholas J. Berry." He'd said all that with a scowl, but it couldn't hold up to Jessica's amused exasperation, and when he grinned back, I was again reminded how great-looking he was.

I had always liked that Nickie/Dickie looked like what he was: a clean-cut, corn-fed midwestern boy. A smokin'-hot midwestern boy, if I may be so uncouth.

Once upon a time his name was Nick, and I'd hoped we'd get naked and make careless reproductive choices together. But when we first met, he saw me as a victim of the crime he hoped to solve (it was a long story involving feral vampires, Kahn's Mongolian BBQ, and my love of garlic). And after he met Jessica, he'd never thought of me at all.

Hmmm. I wasn't sure I liked the way my memories bent. *Memo to me: you have everything. And you're still irked that Nick-Dick never ever saw you in the way you were accustomed. Get over it, you greedy cow.*

Speaking of greedy, was he super-rich in this timeline or struggling on a cop's salary? Which was just pitiful, by the way . . . A good executive assistant made more than the average homicide detective, and admin staff were rarely shot at.

I had it in my head that N-Dick was the heir to the John Deere tractor fortune, but he didn't talk about it much in my old timeline, and frankly, what with my husband being rich and my best friend being rich, I wasn't all that curious about other people's money. In any timeline.

I can hear it now: you're not curious about money because you've always had some! Well. Yeah. I mean, my folks weren't rich or anything—my mom was a teacher, for cripe's sake—but they never wondered if there'd be money left at the end of the month, either. I'm not gonna apologize for being born into the upper-middle class. There were all sorts of more important things to apologize for.

Besides, there was always the chance I had Nick/Dick mixed up with someone else. That happened a lot. Shit, sometimes I got myself mixed up with someone else.

Well! Time to grasp the D-Nick by the horns. There wasn't a subtle or classy way to ask, so . . . "Are you rich right now?"

D-Nick gasped. "You remembered! I am *im*-pressed, oh attentive undead queen with the short-term memory of a tree frog. Half the time you're telling me to dress better, the other half you're telling me it's disgraceful for a trust-fund baby to hog the last of the milk. Time travel has been good for you."

"That's a lie and you know it."

It helped that he was rich, which is why I'd asked; Jess had been screening gold-diggers out of her dating pool since before she graduated high school. In fact, if Nickie/Dickie hadn't been rich, I wondered if their relationship would have come this far.

I couldn't imagine what it would be like to have guys only want you for your money. Pre-Sinclair, most guys only wanted *me* for my terrific tits, and that was enough of a dating burden.

"If we could stay focused," Sinclair suggested, so I quit thinking about Nick's blue-with-flecks-of-gold eyes, his lean and powerful build (shoulders! yowza), and the way he didn't hate me.

"Even for us, we're having trouble staying on track," Marc agreed. "Jesus! How lame are we?"

"Don't take the Lord's name in front of my vampire husband." There was a phrase I couldn't say enough. Sinclair's expression was still frozen in midflinch. "You know it bugs him, and then he bugs me."

"Also," Jessica prompted with a wicked grin, "it's a sin."

"Right! I would have remembered that in a few more minutes. In fact, I—"

The swinging door whooshed open. Which was strange, because most of us were here, and shoving doors open wasn't Tina's style. I'd been so busy yakking I hadn't heard anyone coming down the hall.

"You're back."

I looked up and assumed I was experiencing my first-ever seizure. Great milestone, a personal goal for some time, freak-out induced seizures, woo-hoo! Next, probably my first-ever brain hemorrhage. Then I'd probably need my tonsils out.

Oh, it was going to be a wonderful week.

Standing in the kitchen doorway, looking rumpled and pale and not dead, was one of my dead roommates, Garrett.

And the last time I'd seen *him*, he was in the middle of killing himself.

Did I mentioned he'd succeeded in spectacular fashion?

CHAPTER FIVE

"Gaaaaah," was all I managed as the kitchen floor rushed
up and hit me in the forehead. Stupid rushing floor, why
did it have to move when I'd had a terrible, terrible shock?
Oh, wait. I'd fallen and I couldn't get up. That old lady in
the commercial had a buzzer . . . Where was my buzzer? I
wanted a buzzer. Bring me a buzzer! The queen has spoken.
"Too much . . . weirdness . . . blacking out . . ."

Nick (?) helpfully dripped smoothie on my forehead and
I realized Sinclair was rubbing my hands between his while
Marc tried to check my vitals.

"Why do I always do this?" he bitched. "Why do I ever
try to get a pulse or BP off you?"

"Because you're an idiot in every timeline." I resisted the urge to shout that into the bell of his stethoscope.

"I must apologize." Sinclair's dark eyes were wide. He was rubbing my hands so hard, I assumed he was trying to start a fire. "My poor queen! I should have predicted your reaction."

"Why? When have you *ever* been able to do that? I'm all right." If I had a dollar for every time I ended up ass over teakettle, smack-o on the floor when I was startled or freaked or shot, I'd—well. Since Sinclair's fortune was now mine, I actually did have a dollar for every time. "Let me up."

"No," at least three of them said at once. Then Marc added, "Your pulse is seven. I've mentioned before: that's incompatible with life, right?"

"It's just a lot to take in."

"Tell me! Everything about you is incompatible with life."

"Not my pulse, dumbass. Nick, if you drop one more fruity drop on me—it's in my hair!—I will take you to at least three shoe sales."

He jerked his glass away so quickly he almost dropped it. Ah-ha! So this was a potent weapon in both timelines. Excellent.

One of the worried faces above mine was Garrett's. He looked like he did in my timeline . . . sort of rumpled and fierce, like he could dart off at any moment and his clothes wouldn't hinder him. He was too thin—I always wanted to hook him up to a milkshake IV—and he was sort of flinch-ey.

It's hard to describe . . . he came off as high strung yet calm. Like someone who freaked out at the thought of speaking in public but didn't mind being in a choir. Someone who froze at the thought of back-to-school shopping but didn't mind going to the dentist. Someone who didn't fret about what to wear, but always wore clean clothes.

Garrett was technically an old man—he was an old-timey actor from 1940s Hollywood; how was that for retro?—but his swimmer's build and blond, shoulder-length hair were more *Playgirl* than AARP.

"I made you afraid," he commented, gazing down at me with eyes that were mild as chocolate, yet I remembered times when they could glare with fury.

"You sure did. You've got a lot of nerve being alive." I could hardly believe my eyes. And seeing he had a canvas bag hanging off one shoulder that was stuffed with balls of yarn and bulging with several sizes of knitting needles, I wanted to laugh and give thanks. Garrett, the Fiend formerly known as George, could crochet a mean baby's blanket in this reality as well.

It's corny, but as I reached up to touch his dear face, I felt blessed. I hadn't gotten a chance to know him before he died.

Hadn't bothered, was more like it. And to be honest, my sadness after his suicide had been more guilt than anything else. But I would make up for that. Hadn't I just been thinking about how great it was to get a do-over in Nickie/Dickie's case, how in real life that almost never happened? Here were two, not even five minutes apart.

"I'm so happy to see you. Is—is Antonia . . . ?"

"Yes. She died protecting you. But don't worry, Majesty."

Worry? Was he kidding? I don't think I'd ever been less worried in my life. "Okay."

"You told me your plan."

"I did? How awesome of me. And I know, I'm sure, it was a wonderful plan, a great plan, my most genius plan ever. A plan I was brilliant to think up and you were privileged to hear." I cleared my throat and glared at Jessica and Marc, who were rolling their eyes. "D'you mind reminding me what my plan is?"

"Oh, that. Sure. You and I and the Antichrist are going to hell to get my wife back."

And here it came. Stroke number two.

CHAPTER SIX

"It's not over yet," my dead stepmother warned. **There hadn't** been time to work in a halfway decent insult ("Why can't you go straight to hell like any other decent God-fearing—") before I was shoved so hard, I smacked into the wall and fell.

The impact forced a shower of plaster to rain down on me. There was the deafening boom of a pistol being fired several times over my head. We were trapped in the doorway like ants in a straw. Nobody had any room.

And from that, worse was to come: "Why wasn't she getting up?"

"Twenty-two longs, perfect for the job . . . They ricocheted around her skull but didn't exit . . ."

"But she's a werewolf!"

"Her brains are all over the floor. There will be no coming back from this."

"But she's—she's Antonia! She can't be—I mean, shot?"

"No, she can't be. You're wrong. She's not."

"She jumped in front of me. She saved me."

"Everybody saves you."

And that last flashback quote was still echoing in my head, the way they get all echoey: *saves you, saves you, saves you.*

All that was still thrumming around in my gray matter when the last of the expositional flashback clicked home.

Then we heard the splintering crash come from the stairwell.

I stood, trembling at the silence, and peered into the foyer. I choked back a sob at what Garrett had done to himself.

The regretful Fiend-turned-vampire had kicked the banister off a stretch of curved stairs in the foyer, leaving a dozen or so of the rails exposed and pointing up like spears. Then he had climbed to the second floor to a spot overlooking the stairs and swan dived onto the rails, which had gone through him like teeth.

"See?" my dead stepmother said as we stared down at the second body of a friend in less than a minute. "I warned you."

And the last thing. The last thing I said at the end of that crazy stupid weird scary night.

"It was all just so—so stupid." And preventable, my conscience had whispered. If only you'd been paying attention to business.

And here was the proof! The proof had walked through my kitchen door. The proof was wearing red and white flannel, and carrying a canvas tote bag stuffed with primary colored balls of yarn and knitting needles. I wondered why in *this* timeline, Garrett hadn't killed himself after Antonia died. Did something happen in this timeline's Garrett that made the death of his wife bearable?

"This timeline's Garrett", "that timeline's so-and-so" . . . gaaaaah. I needed an Alternate Timeline vs. Other Timeline scorecard. I was gonna get a headache if I thought it over for too long. And why was I even wondering? Here he was.

Who cared why?

CHAPTER
SEVEN

"Please don't tell me anything new for the next half hour," I begged. I started to lurch to my feet; Sinclair simply grasped my hand and helped me. He was so strong it was like I was floating to my feet. His hand stayed in mine and I squeezed it. He squeezed back.

Okay. This was weird. This was all beyond weird, this was all extremely damned weird, but. But! Everything I'd seen, heard, and felt proved Sinclair and I were in love in this timeline, too. That meant I could . . . I could probably handle any other weirdness as long as I could count on that. *Dear God, THAT WAS NOT A BET. I'm not daring you to freak me out more, God, okay? Okay. You're not to consider that a challenge OF ANY SORT. In Jesus' sake. Amen.*

"How are we supposed to know what you know or don't know?" Marc asked, aggrieved. When I'd pitched out of my chair, my drink had flopped (thick! like Greek yogurt) to the floor. Marc had picked it up, put it in the sink, and was now wiping up the mess.

"I have no idea, but please figure it out this instant." I leaned against Sinclair, which was unnecessary but yummy. That boy was built like a barn door, all broad and hard.

Barn door? I must have hit my head harder than I thought. There was nothing sexy about a barn door. Unless I was jammed up against it while Sinclair played pirate (the swash-buckling kind from the 1700s, not the icky Somalian kind from right now).

". . . help me?"

"Huh?" Okay. No time to think of pirates. Time to focus. "Sorry, I didn't catch that."

"When will you be prepared to help me?" Garrett asked again.

"Good question. Okay. Let's figure this out. My big new plan was for you and me to go to hell," I prompted him, "so we can get your wife."

He nodded. He was still carrying his tote o' knitting supplies, and it was super cute.

"Your wife . . . who is dead now. Here," I clarified, "in this timeline."

He nodded again. Ahhh, Garrett, how it all came back to me . . . like how he never talked. Shit, for the first few months he lived here, he *couldn't* talk. But he fed on my blood, and the blood of the Antichrist (long story) and remembered all sorts of things. Like how to talk. And crochet baby blankets. And knit sweaters. He made a black sweater with yellow piping for Sinclair last year. My husband wore it once but, when I collapsed into laughter and spent the afternoon calling him Bee Man, never wore it again.

"Why do you think Antonia's in hell?"

Garrett blinked, surprised. Then, "Where else *would* she be?"

I thought about Antonia's near-constant pissy mood, her fuming anger, which was occasionally overtaken by spitting rage. Her standard greeting ("What's up, dumbasses?") and her standard farewell ("Bye, losers.").

"Right. Right! Good thinking, Garrett. You're a man of few words and *mucho* brains in both universes. So, your dead wife is in hell. And you want to go get her, like an Orpheus thing?"

My husband's eyebrows arched. "My love, you never cease to amaze. You know of Orpheus and Eurydice?"

"Duh, Sink Lair."

"Wonderful," he muttered. "Another dreadful holdover through both timelines?"

"Yeah, well, in both timelines your secret name is Sink Lair, and I'm a total badass when it comes to Greek mythology."

"It's true," Jessica told N/Dick. "She's won contests. She's won Trivial Pursuit tournaments."

"It's fascinating, once you get over the ick factor of all of them marrying their brothers and sisters. And killing their dads. Anyway. So you want to go to hell to bring Antonia back here. Even though she's dead."

"You will fix it," Garrett said firmly. I was both flattered and horrified by his faith in me. "You are the queen. And you also know Greek mythology."

"And I agreed to this?"

"Yes."

It sounded authentic. I wasn't exactly known for my careful deliberation and cautious tactics. Assuming we could even find Antonia, could we bring a dead person out of hell and back to earth?

Never mind: I'd said I would do it. And I was a woman of my word in every universe, dammit. "Uh . . . so we, what? Pack a lunch? And then I, what? Summon Satan?"

Silence, though I could almost hear the clicking eyeballs as we all stared at each other. Nobody said anything. Which, for this group, was scary and weird.

After a long moment of stare downs: "Maybe you could just call the Antichrist on her cell first," Jessica suggested.

"Yes! Excellent plan. Much better than sacrificing shoes."

"What?"

"I don't want to talk about it," I said in my best I-don't-want-to-talk-about-it tone. Some things were just too painful to discuss, even with my best (fat) friend.

"And I am not fat!" she cried, reading my mind in the way only a best friend can, which never failed to make me feel cared for yet freaked out. Two people knew what I was thinking most of the time: one of them was the richest woman in Minnesota, and the other one was a dead farmer. These are the things I faced weekly, if not daily.

"Well, you certainly aren't—ow!" I stared at Sinclair. "Did you . . . did you just grab my ear and yank?"

"I tripped," the king of the vampires responded, suaver than usual.

"And your finger fell on my ear and pulled it?"

"If you were about to say 'you certainly aren't thin,' then he saved your unworthy white butt, because I would have cut your ear *off* your *head*!"

"She would have," D/Nick said, nodding hard. "The hormones, Betsy. You have no idea. It's a rare week when she doesn't cut something off somebody."

"Gross," was my only comment.

"Are you going to call the Antichrist or not?"

"Don't call her," a new voice answered. Just what we needed . . . a new, sneaky vampire.

And everything went from sucky to beyond sucky, if there was such a thing.

Who am I kidding? Of course there was.

CHAPTER
EIGHT

I know why I assumed it was a vampire. Sneaking up on me is easy. Sneaking up on Sinclair, not so much. So I think it's fair to say I knew what I was getting into when I sprinted toward it.

All I could think was, *Dick isn't carrying, and neither is Nick. Marc smells like blood . . . stupid scrubs! And Jessica . . . my God, Jessica and the baby . . . her enormous fat unborn baby . . . oh Jesus . . .*

So I was out for blood the minute my big white butt was out the door. Except so was the bad guy, because although I was moving pretty quickly, he managed to grab my shoulders and shove me back, so hard and fast I couldn't even get a glimpse of his face in the shadows of the long hallway.

I flew down the hall—like Supergirl! And crashed through a wall that was, luckily for me, over a hundred years old. Yerrggh, the smell of mouse poop was almost enough to distract me from the stabbing pain of my newly cracked ribs.

A low chuckle out of the gloom. "Don't worry. It won't leave a mark."

Jessica . . . the baby . . .

I crawled out of mouse poop, plaster, lath, and dust and stumbled . . . I'd been thrown so hard I'd been knocked out of my shoes. I abandoned them without a thought—

(Oh, my poor scuffed Beverly Feldmans! Pal, you are so GONNA DIE!)

—and ran past the door to the attic and back down the hall. Nothing good ever came out of the attic, and I was going to amend that to *nothing good ever came out of the attic or the hallway near the attic*. Whatever-it-was had lurked in that hallway, the longest one in the house, listening in on our conversation and smoothie-snorting. Creepy *and* lame.

"Okay. Let's try that again." That sounded cool and brave, right? Not at all like I was scared shitless, right? Excellent.

"Okayyyyyyyyyyy."

I could almost see him in the gloom . . . and I was *reminded* of someone. There was something about the line of the jaw . . . too bad this was all happening at super-hypersonic speed, instead of real time. If I had five minutes,

I'd be able to sit down and figure this out. I was not, at the best of times, a fast thinker.

"Hope you're ready for round two, bitch!" Which sounded much more badass in my head than out loud. I could never pull off the generic "the price is wrong, bitch!" vulgarity. "Don't be fooled if I didn't sound as badass as I could have. You're about to get a face full of badass! *Then* you'll be sorry."

That's when somebody grabbed my sweater (argh! A gift from Jess . . . red cashmere!) and hauled me backward. I again flew through the air with the greatest of ease, at what I assumed was the speed of sound, but didn't break anything on this landing. Woo-hoo! In fact, I'd mostly slid along the highly waxed mellowly aged floors.

That's when I realized: Sinclair had grabbed me and jerked me out of harm's way. That was my husband in a nutshell: he'd commit felony assault on me. To save me!

"If this were the kind of movie my wife enjoys," Sinclair said coldly, standing—looming, really—and almost entirely blocking the doorway, "I would make an inane announcement. Something silly and time-wasting like, 'if you touch my wife again, I will kill you.' Except you did touch my wife. And I *am* going to kill you. Because no one gets a chance to hurt her twice."

"Really?" There was obvious delight in the thing's voice. "Will you really? You'll kill me? That would be woooooonderful." Then, lower and much more sly: "Betsy, I seeeeee youuuuuuuu."

"Who the *hell*—" Marc began. Dick had managed to keep Jessica in the kitchen, but he'd had no luck with Marc, who wasn't above a knee in the 'nads to get from point A to point B. His lust for excitement had gotten him into jams worse than this.

Seeing Marc alive and well socked the memory home for me; I knew who our unwelcome visitor was.

"Do you seeeee meeeeee?"

The Marc Thing, from the future. Somehow he'd followed Laura and me back to the present. And now he was in my house.

Shit.

CHAPTER
NINE

"Following me back was a bad idea," I told the Marc Thing as I manfully cradled my cracked ribs. "The sort of idea that will get you staked a zillion times in the balls."

"Don't tease," it said.

I glanced at Marc. His color was high; he had a look of avid curiosity on his face. He smelled like—it's hard to explain; he smelled like hot wiring. You know how you sometimes taste metal when you get an adrenaline rush? He smelled like how that tastes. Excited. A little afraid. But not enough afraid, and was that a good thing or a bad thing?

How to explain this to him? *Say, Marc, in the future I turned into Supremo Bitch-o of North America and tortured you for decades—after not saving you from being killed, oopsie!—until*

*you went batshit nuts and now the you from the future is here to
do all sorts of disgusting things to all of us, which is all my fault.
Sorry. I owe you one, okay?*

"My queen is quite correct . . . you will be staked. Only
not in the balls." We all jumped; I jumped and groaned . . .
reeeally wish the cracked ribs would heal already. Tina, one
of the awesomest vampires I knew (I didn't know very many
awesome vampires; shame it was such a short list) had snuck
up on the Marc Thing and stuck the barrel of her 9mm
Beretta in his ear.

"Wonderful," the Marc Thing and Marc said in unison,
which was just creepy.

It always surprised me to see Tina wielding firearms; she
was an expert with all sorts of guns and had been ever since
I'd known her.

Because she'd been born, or died, or whatever, during the
Civil War, I was always amazed to see her handling modern
weaponry. Which was dumb . . . it wasn't like I expected
to see her running around in hoopskirts brandishing mint
juleps. Such a capricious nature has man. Or something.

Tina always looked good, but tonight she looked like an
angel. And could have passed for one—she'd been killed
in her late teens, or early twenties . . . something like that.
Who can keep track of when everybody died? Anyway, she
was mega-gorgeous, with a gorgeous fall of shiny blond hair

and the biggest, prettiest brown eyes I'd ever seen. Pansy eyes, my mom called them.

"Have I mentioned," Sinclair began, smiling for the first time since the Marc Thing made his presence known, "that I adore having you around?"

"Oh yes, my king. You are good enough to make frequent mention of it."

"*You're* not *really* theeeeeere," the Marc Thing sang. He acted like standing in a hostile house surrounded by enemies, and with an earful of gun, was all in a day's work. Which it prob'ly was.

"On your knees. Slowly, if you please. And . . . yes." Tina kept the barrel of the gun socked tightly in his ear as she bent at the knees to accommodate the Marc Thing getting on his. "Now on your stomach. Yes." Sinclair shifted so his foot was resting lightly on the Marc Thing's wrist. My husband smiled pleasantly at the Marc Thing, who leered back, and everyone in the hall knew that if the Marc Thing even twitched, Sinclair would grind his wrist into splintered bone. Which made it safe for Tina to pull back and step back. Still: maybe next time Sinclair should rest his foot on its neck. Call me hospitable.

For the first time I realized Garrett had also come out of the kitchen, which was something of a shock. In my timeline, Garrett had been a wreck, a shell, a disaster of a man.

A coward, but not without reason. He'd been murdered, then driven insane, then murdered some more . . . and in my timeline, it drove him to suicide.

"Uh, maybe you should go back in the kitchen and keep an eye on Dee-Nick and Jessica. Back in the kitchen. And not in here."

"Dee-Nick sent me out here." Garrett correctly read my look of surprise, because he lifted his left shoulder in a slight shrug and added, "Antonia died right in front of me. There's nothing to be scared of now."

He was wrong, of course. But I didn't have the heart to disabuse him of that sorry-ass notion. He was almost a hundred years old, but I'd always felt older than him in both timelines.

CHAPTER
TEN

I caught Sinclair's eye and tipped my head to the left, indicating another hallway. Before things went even thirty seconds further, I had to talk to my husband.

"Tina, if you please."

"Of course."

"Garrett—"

"Yes, King Sinclair."

King Sink Lair. Hee! It wasn't the time or place (it so rarely was) but I couldn't swallow my giggle. There was an annoying amount of *my king* and *Your Majesty* and *dread king*, but I didn't think anyone had ever used *King Sinclair* in my hearing.

"I shall not even ask why you found that amusing," he

sighed as we stepped into the darkened hallway. "Are you well, my own? Not hurt, yes?"

"Not hurt, no. Okay. Real quick, because I don't like being out of the sight line of that crazy fuck . . . one of the skatey-eight zillion things I haven't had a chance to tell you about Laura and Betsy's Time Travel Follies is that we went to the future, too, a thousand years in the future, and in that future Ancient Betsy tortured Marc for decades and drove him insane."

Sinclair's composure, as much a part of him as his Cole Haan loafers and big dick, slipped, and he stared at me with wide eyes and a shocked expression.

And I was ashamed . . . more than I had ever been in my life. Ashamed that I was capable of that, that I could grow into someone who could/would do that to Marc. And ashamed that, now, Sinclair knew, too. He wouldn't be the last person I told, either . . . I'd have to warn everyone. I'd have to let my friends and family know about the awful thing I hadn't done yet. Just when I thought their opinion of me couldn't plummet further . . .

"I-I thought you should know." I shook my head and stared at the floor. It was very hard to look my husband in the eyes just now. "I didn't want to tell you."

"No. I imagine you didn't." He put a finger beneath my chin and raised my head. "Do you know, I haven't been afraid of anyone until you cured Jessica's cancer? After my twin was murdered, I feared nothing. I *felt* nothing. Now the only thing I fear is you. I shall pause so you can make a sarcastic observation."

"And a smoothie made with frozen, not fresh, strawberries! And having someone fill up your Jaguar with regular unleaded, not premium!" It nearly burst out of me. He knew me so well. "You're afraid of lots of things."

"Yes, thank you for comparing my fear to petrol. I don't mind, you know."

I was getting that surreal am-I-drunk-or-just-weirded-out feeling. "Don't mind what?"

"Being afraid of you. Well. I *mind*, but it doesn't prey on me. And the reason it doesn't—"

"Maybe we should be getting back in there with Marc and the Marc Thing and the others." How long had we been yakking in this secluded hall, anyway? Time was a-wastin'.

"—is because I love you more than I fear you."

"Okay." That didn't seem adequate, so I added, "Thanks. I think you're neat-o, too."

Sinclair rubbed his forehead with a familiar I'm-getting-a-migraine-and-want-to-shoot-someone expression. "Frightened of an idiot; it is a shameful, shameful day for the House of Sinclair."

"The *House* of *Sinclair*?" I shrieked. Lame! So completely fully utterly laaaaaame! "House of Sinclair! Oh, that's a riot. What's our family crest, a cross with the international symbol for No slashed across it? A blender wrought in gold leaf?"

"Thank you as always for your courteous attention and appropriate commentary." He grabbed my wrist, swung around, and back to the kitchen we went.

CHAPTER
ELEVEN

Nickie-Dickie-Tavvie (best Rudyard Kipling story ever) held
a gun on the Marc Thing while Tina taped him to the fridge.
I was gripping the cross on my necklace . . . one twitch, and
maybe not even one, and I was gonna jam it through his
forehead.

I had to stare for a good thirty seconds to understand
what I was seeing. I thought the hallway had been surreal?
Sinclair was right; I *was* an idiot. (He was also a jerk: who
calls the awesome and only love of his life an idiot? Note
to me: jerk his testicles up to his nostrils, then twist. Then
nobly accept his apology. Repeat.)

Tina had yanked the fridge out from the wall and
unplugged it. She'd found several rolls of duct tape—you

know how most people have a junk drawer in their kitchen? Yeah, well, in our Green Mill–sized kitchen, we had a junk cabinet, and in that cabinet were many rolls of duct tape. (Also many rolls of regular tape, index cards, Post-its, pens and pencils, markers, string—who used string anymore?— and various envelopes. And that was only the first shelf.)

Old vampires like Tina and Sinclair loved duct tape. Loooooooved it. They didn't like just using it for what it was intended (e.g., fixing, repairing, undoing), they *made* things out of it. Pretty much any vampire born before duct tape had been invented thought it was the coolest stuff on earth. Velcro-cool. IPod cool.

Anyway, Tina was taping the Marc Thing to the fridge. And doing it at ramped-up vampire speed. So what I saw was basically a blur of Tina spooling tape all over the Marc Thing like Charlotte spewed web for Wilbur. Which the Marc Thing found hilarious.

It was all surreal enough to almost make me forget the pain of my mashed ribs. Which, to be honest, were feeling better and better. I hadn't had any blood in—what century was I in? Okay, not quite right, I'd munched a bit on Sinclair before all the madness started (again), but it wasn't the first time I noticed I was needing less blood and healing faster.

Something to wonder about, some *other* time.

"You'd be surprised," Dickie/Nickie was telling Jessica, who looked as fascinated as I felt. "You can't break it—most people can't break it, and look how many rolls she's going through!—and you can't untie it. It's as good as rope made out of Holy Water."

"The things I learn when I've been knocked up," she commented.

"So many questions," Marc agreed, "and none of them are tape-related."

"I have questions for youuuuuu, tooooo," the Marc Thing hummed.

"Ech, why do you talk like that?" Jessica asked. "Are you trying to come off as batshit crazy?"

"That is what I was going for, Big Round Jessica," he confessed, "yes."

"I guess I should defend your honor," Nickie/Dickie/Tavvie said doubtfully, "but how? Kick him? Shoot him? Can I get a stake through all that tape?"

"Save that for later," Sinclair said. He was watching the blur of Tina and tape with approval. Then he turned back to the Marc Thing. "Unchivalrous comments aside, perhaps I won't kill you."

It pouted, which was not a pretty sight. "Spoilsport."

"I will, however, require information."

"I require it, too," Marc added, and Jess and N/Dick both nodded.

I didn't . . . I required him to die, leave, burst into flames, or turn into a new pair of Beverly Feldmans. But I had the feeling I wasn't going to get what I wanted, at least right away. It wasn't the first time no one gave a tin shit for my opinion. Queen-schmeen.

Sinclair glanced at our friends with an expression we'd all seen before, because Jessica jumped right in. "Don't you start pulling that only-vampires-can-know-about-this crap, Sink Lair."

My husband closed his eyes and rubbed his eyelids. He looked like the Before picture in a Pepto-Bismol commercial. "Please don't pronounce my name like that."

"Because we all live here; you're not in this alone! Yeah, we're not vampires—"

"Not yet," Marc Thing said slyly, earning him a sharp rap on the top of his head ("Hey!") from Tina. If I were him, I wouldn't antagonize Tina any further . . . the next smack could cave in his skull.

"—but it affects us, it affects all of us, the living and the undead, landlord *and* tenants."

"Not that you let any of us pay rent," N/Dick pointed

out with a dammit-I'm-a-man-not-a-consort expression. "So you can't shut us out this time, Sinclair."

Sinclair's eyes opened slowly, like a lizard's. "Can't?"

Jessica faltered for a second; her hand went to her gruesomely massive stomach and rubbed . . . I would have bet a thousand dollars that she wasn't aware of it. "Shouldn't. You shouldn't shut us out, is what we meant."

"Where have you even been?" I asked Tina, who was using the last of the seventh roll. "I forgot you were even in the house until you rode in like Marshal Dillon in a pastel green T-shirt."

"Waiting for you and the king to finish your lovemaking." Tina smiled and brushed duct-fuzz from her perfect green shirt. Green was excellent on most blondes, and super-excellent on her. She looked like a sexy leprechaun. "I imagined that, once you renewed affectionate relations—"

"I'm not having this conversation," I decided.

"—you would debrief His Majesty."

"Oh." Marc coughed. "Is that what the kids are calling it these days?"

"You guys, let's not get sidetracked by my sex life," I begged.

"Usually you can time it," Jessica said as they all (!) nodded with intent expressions. "They reunite, they bang, they talk, they bang again, they get thirsty, they make smoothies, we know it's safe to get close."

"None of that is so bad," N/Dick said, "but they don't stick to their bedroom. Shit, last week I was minding my own business, looking for the weed whacker—I know it's November, somebody please tell that to the weeds by the back gate—and they were doing it in the damn shed! I'll never look at bags of fertilizer the same way again."

"And now, neither will any of us," Marc said.

"You guys," I pleaded. Unfortunately, he had me there. And even if he didn't, Marc had walked in on Sinclair and me not even three hours ago. (I'd been very, very, very, very, very glad to return from hell and reunite with my husband.) "You can't blame us for occasionally following our instincts."

"Why do your instincts involve sex and rooms that people normally would not have sex in?"

"If you go into the basement," Garrett said, "you can barely hear them, and if you go into the tunnel you can't hear them at all."

"That's a good idea! I'll remember that," Jessica said, and Dickie/Nickie nodded.

Incredibly, Tina was also nodding. Like this wasn't a bizarro conversation. Like this was a normal thing in their lives. "I shall as well. But as I was explaining, I was waiting for Their Majesties to finish—it was the third time this week, so going by their pattern in the past—"

"We should make a chart," N/Dick said.

"That would be easier—you could just see at a glance—"

"And you'd know which areas on the property to avoid!"

"We're not having this conversation!"

A short, sudden silence, broken by the Marc Thing: "It seems as though we are."

I pinched the bridge of my nose. "Shut up, you crazy fucking psycho vampire weirdo."

"Ouch," it said mildly. "Words can hurt, too, Vampire Queen."

CHAPTER
TWELVE

"Before things go any further, we need to call Laura."

"Good idea," I replied. "We were going to anyway, because of . . ." I eyed the Marc Thing. Why give the psycho more info than we had to? "Because of the errand I need to run later."

"Don't you remember? You're not very bright in this century, but don't let that shame you for even a moment," the Marc Thing soothed. His tone didn't match his expression, so it was like being soothed by a rattlesnake. A creepy, well-dressed rattlesnake who would bite you, and be sorry after. Maybe. Needless to say, I wasn't soothed. "You need your sister to take you to hell."

"Anyway." I glared. The Marc Thing smirked. I wondered

if Advil would work on a vampire. I was getting a real bitch-kitty of a tension headache. Maybe a hundred Advil? Actually, since we weren't really prone to that sort of thing, my headache was likely psychological. How is it that, even if you know it's all in your head, it still hurts? "We were going to reach out to her anyway." I fumbled around in my pants for a good thirty seconds before I realized I must have lost my cell phone. Maybe . . . ?

My husband reached into his suit coat, extracted my phone, and silently (yet suavely) held it out to me. I had a dim memory of bursting, Hulk-like, out of my leggings a couple hours earlier when my cell phone flew with the greatest of ease . . . never mind. "Nobody say anything," I warned, and stabbed the button for Laura.

"Wouldn't dream of it," Marc assured me.

"Me, either!" the Other Marc said.

"It's ringing, it's—"

"Hello?"

"Oh, good, your cell works in hell."

"Betsy!" My sister sounded vaguely pleased. Well, just vague. Probably more distracted than anything else. "I'm heading to Goodwill . . . I've got a box of summer clothes I want to give away."

I was taken aback by the mental image her statement conjured up. "They have Goodwill in hell?"

"I'm not *in* hell. I'm in Apple Valley."

"Oh. Okay." I let pass all the comments I could make about Apple Valley, which was a perfectly nice Twin Cities suburb if you liked cities with no personality of their own. "When did you get back?"

"I . . . I'm just back now."

Weird. Was she trying my patience, or my temper? What was up with the vagueness? Oh, the hell with it. I had other fish to et cetera. "Listen, something's come up and I really, really, really need you to come over as soon as you can."

"Twenty minutes," she promised, and clicked off.

"Twenty minutes," I told them.

"What shaaaaaall we do until then?" the Marc Thing sang. He was made immobile by all the tape, but the creepy animation in his cold, cold face was jarring to say the least.

"We could take turns shooting you," N/Dick said. There was real distaste in his voice, and I couldn't blame him. Talking to the Marc Thing was like having a conversation with someone you couldn't see but knew would bite you if he got the chance. It was like being trapped in an elevator with a great white shark. Who had live grenades taped to his fin. And a toothache, which didn't help his mood. Baaaad shit.

"I am prepared—dying, really, no pun intended—fully prepared to undergo a grueling interrogation and scream out answers from a throat full of black blood."

"Jeez," Jessica complained, "do you have to?"

"Who killed me? And why? And what happened after? And why? And why did I follow you and the Anti-Laura back? And how? And how do I get my hair to look so good a thousand years in the past? I am," he said, looking around the kitchen, "surrounded by primitives. Not to mention primitive hair and skin-care products. Just because I don't have to shave doesn't mean I don't want to smell and look terrific. I can't remember the last time I . . ." His gaze had been darting around and his eyes reminded me of a weasel's . . . alert and mean . . . and hungry . . . at the same time.

But when he glanced out the kitchen window into the star-filled night, the nasty/fun tone went out of his voice and he just stared out the window for the next minute—I timed him, like Madonna timed Tom Hanks peeing in *A League of Their Own*, without saying anything.

Tina let out a delicate fake-cough to get his attention. "Oh, look. We're being dreadful hosts."

"Dreadful," Sinclair agreed, sounding about as interested as a corpse. Which he sort of—yeesh, never mind.

"Perhaps after our discussion you might like to go outside," she offered.

Awesome. That girl is smart. That girl who is almost two hundred years old is *super* smart. Me, I would have threatened him with a chain-saw nose job, followed by a lawn mower enema, but Tina instantly saw one of his weaknesses and moved in. You couldn't teach that stuff, man. That shit had to be innate.

"It's supposed to rain later," she continued, sauntering across the room until she was leaning against the sink with the big window right behind her. "We *are* having an unseasonably mild November."

N/Dick and Jessica and I all fell all over ourselves agreeing with her—my, yes, super unseasonable, unbelievably unseasonable, and the most beauteous November any of us could remember in the last thirty years because it was just all so gorgeous and cool and we wanted to go outside, too! Jeepers, maybe, when certain unpleasant interrogations were over, maybe we could *all* go outside! How cool would that be?

"Do you remember," she asked kindly, "how the air smells just before it rains?"

"No," it said shortly, and it didn't say another word until Laura showed. That was a long seventeen minutes.

CHAPTER
THIRTEEN

A word about vampire superpowers: mostly I don't notice them. (This actually explains many things in my life. I'm too busy livin', baby! Who has time to contemplate every damn thing? Life is for living! And gobs of sex.) That probably sounds strange, because I haven't been undead very long. But it's true. After a while you realize you were bitching about somebody snoring . . . and they were doing it seventeen rooms and three floors away. Or you'll whine about food going bad . . . and the garbage was already triple bagged and taken out into a sealed-off garage.

It's scary how fast you get used to it. These days I took it for granted almost all the time. Like lumpless gravy. (It's surprisingly easy.) But tonight I was listening hard, so even though we were all still in the kitchen, I heard Laura's little sewing machine engine–powered Kia pull in.

"She's here," Sinclair and I said in unison. Tina, who must have known, hadn't taken her gaze off the Marc Thing. If that bothered him, he didn't let on. It probably took a lot more than an eyeballing from Tina to scare someone who used to have a Caesar haircut and was tortured for decades.

Jessica and Marc both jumped. "That's creepy," Jessica said. "And it always, always will be."

"Yeah, knock it off," Marc added.

"Children, children," the Marc Thing said, still staring out the window.

"Tell me she's not still driving that Kia," N/Dick begged.

"Who cares?" I asked. "You've got something against good gas mileage?"

"It's the Soul," he explained. "Kia's new miniwagon is called the Soul."

"Oh, lame!" This time I had spoken in unison with the Marc Thing, which was beyond blech. "Get your own lines," I hissed to him. To the others: "That's just bad. Lame, and bad. And lame! The Soul. Please. We don't have enough problems? The Soul."

"We've had this conversation before," D/Nick reminded me.

"Well, I don't remember it, so back off." As if I didn't have waaaay more important things to remember than keeping track of Laura's vehicles. Well, I did, dammit. In my old timeline, Laura's dad had saved for over a year to get her that Kia, which she loved almost as much as I loved new Manolos. Her adopted dad, is what I meant; her real dad, also my dad, was dead.

Wait, was he? Maybe in this timeline, he and (barf) my stepmonster, Antonia, were alive! And yes! I know how silly it is to have two people in the same house with the same weird name! So shut up!

How could I find out? Sure, everyone in the room knew what a moron I was, but that didn't mean I, you know, was in a big hurry to reinforce and advertise it. Was there a way to just casually ask, "So, is my dad alive?"

The kitchen door swung open, and in came the Antichrist. "Goodwill used to be more grateful," she said by greeting. "Now they're more interested in paperwork over polite conversation."

"Thanks for coming so—"

"Twice! I've worn those jeans twice! Not a speck of paint, which is no mean feat when you paint in them. I thought it'd be nice to give away clothing that was only 'gently used' as opposed to falling off me in shreds. Any gratitude, though? Hmm? Not a thanks, not even a smile."

"Here's the thing," I tried again.

Laura was shaking her perfectly coiffed hair out of her

gorgeous eyes. "Just 'do you want a slip for your taxes?' No I do *not*, but how about some eye contact?" Laura was a luscious blonde . . . close to my height, give or take an inch, with beautiful blue eyes, a perfect pink-hued complexion, and a gorgeous fall of corn-silk blond hair. Just . . . sickening.

"I'm here," she said unnecessarily. "What's—oh, God!" She was pointing at The Thing That Was Jessica's Gut, and I couldn't blame her. "What—are you—what *is* that?"

"You haven't noticed any subtle and not so subtle weirdnesses—"

"Is that even a word?"

"Shut up, Marc or Marc Thing." I hadn't been looking, I was embarrassed to say. That sly/sneaky tone could have come from either the live Marc or the dead one. Because I didn't. Have enough. Problems.

"How long were you home? How's your mom—not the devil, your other mom? Has she had a perm? Quit school? Or never went to college? Do you have another sibling? New pets? Are old dead pets alive again? Is your dad—your live one, not our dead one—still a minister? That"—I pointed, ignoring Jessica's glare—"is the least of the scary-ass goings-on around here. Here, Dick and Jess are practically married, and are practicing living happily ever after."

Laura rounded on me like a gunfighter, using shrill accusations as bullets. On the whole, I'd have preferred actual lead bullets. "It's because you didn't feed on Nick when we were in the past! You fed on me instead, you thoughtless starving wretch!"

"Ouch," I said mildly.

"I warned you! Didn't I warn you?"

"You were less shrill in the old timeline."

"That changed his future, and Jessica's!"

"You don't have to make it sound like a bad thing."

"Excuse me!" Jessica's Sperm Boy was waving his arms around. "First off, it's Dick. I hate Nick, I've hated it my entire life," Nick said. "Second, *didn't* feed on him? Could the studio audience hear the playback on that one, please?"

"No time. I'll get you the blog entry later. Laura, the reason we called you here—"

"I don't know nothin' 'bout birthin' no babies."

"Cliché!" I said, clenching a fist in triumph. "That's been used to death in several sitcoms, including *Night Court*. *Night Court*, Laura. Be ashamed."

"Except I do," Laura said, calming down a little. "When our ministry spent a summer in Malawi, we assisted at dozens of births. There are at least three Lauras in Malawi, the moms were *so* nice and grateful."

"Getting gratitude is becoming a thing with you, but even so, you're the worst Antichrist ever," Jessica said. "Which is actually comforting. Stay close."

"It's not why you're here."

"Too bad." Laura sighed. "It would have been neat to deliver a baby. That tends to be the opposite of evil."

"Depends on the baby," Marc muttered.

"Cheer up—anything can happen in the next few weeks. Fairfield Hospital . . . the devil's daughter . . . if you *don't* have to deal with an HMO it's almost worth it . . ." Being dead was good for that if nothing else. Never again would I get a whopping bill because I'd dared use the gynecologist I was most comfortable with. "Sorry, you have to use our guy or we'll charge you a zillion bucks." Talk about soulless.

But! Enough musing about HMOs; I felt we were getting off track. This was nothing new, just alarming. Time was not on our side . . . even though I had a time-traveling sister.

"Laura, listen. You know all those cute stories about people moving and then their pets following them across the country to the new house? Or a kitten takes a liking to a family and follows them around until they give in and feed it before the ASPCA gets involved, and the new family ends up taking care of it so it doesn't go feral and kill everyone in the neighborhood?" I gestured to the trussed Marc Thing. "Guess what followed us back?"

"OhdearGod," Laura said, and missed when she reached out to grasp the back of a kitchen chair to steady herself.

Her arms pinwheeled for a hilarious second until N/Dick reached out to steady her.

"Well put."

"How did I not notice he was sitting *right there?*"

"I was wondering that, too," Tina admitted.

"The gut," she replied absently. "I'm not used to Jessica weighing more than seventy-eight pounds. I couldn't help be mesmerized by it. I couldn't *not* look at it."

"No one can not look at it," I soothed, ignoring Jessica's glare.

"Oooh, yuck!"

"Disgusting," I agreed.

"I'm sitting"—the Marc Thing sighed—"right here."

"We actually weren't talking about—" I began, but fortunately wiser heads than mine (that would be every head in the room) were better able to stay on track.

"This isn't . . . *our* fault?" Laura looked horrified.

"Only in that I was able to follow you back to your loved ones because you burst onto my timeline with no right or invitation, after gaily running amok in my past *and* yours and instigating catastrophic change in the very fabric of the universe."

"Anything sounds bad when you put it like that," I snapped. Then, "Wait. How did you know we'd been in the past before falling into the future?"

"*You* told me," the Marc Thing replied.

I hate time travel.

"Why haven't we killed him yet?" N/Dick asked. As a cop, this wasn't an idle question. "He's already dead, so I can probably keep us out of trouble. And he's only here to fuck us or kill us."

"Or kill us and fuck us," Laura said. That was somewhat out of character, and from Sinclair's surprised glance, I wasn't the only one who thought so.

"I'm going to do a quick sweep around the house, make sure he didn't sprinkle any other surprises around before he let you grab him," Laura said, and darted off.

"Okay, that was . . . heroic, I think." Though what Laura would know about sneakiness that Sinclair and Tina wouldn't . . . oh, who cared? Back to business.

"Shall we kill him?" Tina was saying. "We could empty a clip into his head or put that shiny new axe to use—the one I ordered from Cabela's?—and chop him up into many, many pieces, or bleed him out and then set the corpse—"

"Uggghh," Jessica said, and rapidly waddled from the room, both hands crammed over her lips. Her eyes were practically bulging out of her head, and I knew exactly how she felt.

"—or burn him with acid or tie weights to all his pieces and drop him in lakes all over the world and be done with it."

"That sounds extreme," I said, and it was a sorry-ass day when I was the voice of reason. "It's not really our thing."

"But you know he isn't here to help us. Come on, really? He's come all this way to *not* hideously murder us in a number of gruesome ways?" Dee/Nick asked. "You've seen vengeance flicks, right?"

"Point," Tina admitted.

"I've gotta think about more than my safety, or yours," he continued as we all tried not to hear Jessica throwing up in the small bathroom down the hall. "I don't think it's a good idea to just stand around talking about this. We need to make a decision and then get it done."

Wow. I was still having trouble getting used to Nick/Dick liking me again, never mind him using his awesome cop-powers to keep us safe, or out of trouble.

The Marc Thing seemed pretty cool about his impending dismemberment. "Don't you want to hear my unexpected-yet-vital information that will change the course of your lives?" it asked.

"No/Uh-uh/Not really," Tina, Dick, and I said at the same time.

And whoa! Dee-Nick *and* Tina had produced guns from nowhere. "How many bullets will it take?" Nee-Dick asked.

"Shall we find out?" Tina said.

"Everything looks fine," Laura announced, coming back into the kitchen. "I don't think—whoa!" She took in the scene: Sinclair and me silently looking on, Tina and Nickie/Dickie making like two of the Charlie's Angels, and a greenish Jessica staggering down the hallway. "Okay. What'd I miss? And Tina, how many guns do you have?"

"Seventy-four. And let's be honest. First, it's a safety issue. Second, it's what he wants—"

"Yes, yes, yesssss!" The Marc Thing was too thoroughly taped to bounce, but he wriggled happily. It was like watching a worm trying to do the Forbidden Dance. "I do, I do, I really, really do! Ah, Laura, truly the spawn of angels . . . one angel, anyway, I dooooo!"

"Ick," Laura commented. Then, "So it's like Tina said? It's what he wants and it's a good way to keep all of us safe so we should feel good about killing him and just get it over with?"

Jessica had almost made it back to the kitchen when we heard her turn around to return to the bathroom. Cue ralphing noises.

"So just . . . *sayonara*, sucker, and ka-blam?" D/Nick asked, looking doubtful. He'd made a gun from his thumb and forefinger (dumb, since he had *an actual* gun on the Marc Thing) and looked down at it with less than perfect confidence. "He's a pretty old vampire. I don't think it'll be simple."

"*Mucho* ka-blam will be required," the Marc Thing agreed, then pouted. "It's not nice to throw my age in my face. I'd never do that to you, Nick."

"Shut up," he replied absently. "Okay, sounds like we're on the same page. Funny how when I got up this morning I figured Lamaze class would be stressful and bloody." We all heard the click of the hammer dropping. "Let's—"

"Right here in our very own kitchen? We eat smoothies in here! And since when are *you* so quick to not follow any of the cop rules?"

"Since I moved in with vampires and knocked up your best friend?" Nick replied, like it was a quiz.

"We can still have smoothies in here," Laura soothed. "We'll just mop. A lot."

I glanced at my sister. She was taking this awfully well. Laura usually wouldn't get on board for baiting mouse traps, never mind kitchen executions. Oh, sure, she sometimes snapped and murdered serial killers and vampires, and she had tons of devil-worshipping followers who would kill or die for her, but on the whole, she was in the Murder Is Bad category. "You're taking this—" I began.

"Wait!"

We waited. When Sinclair used that tone, everybody played Statues. Even if I was half an inch from orgasm, it was Statue City. The opposite, if you're wondering, of romantic.

"Marc?"

"Yes?" they both replied.

"The undead one," Sinclair clarified. "You called him Nick."

"Even as a sprat, your hearing is excellent."

"Why did you do that?"

N/Dick started to open his mouth, but Sinclair made a curt motion with the flat of his hand.

"Because . . . it's . . . his name?" the Marc Thing wondered, gazing at the ceiling.

"Not here it isn't," Tina said, her big eyes going all badass narrow. This was a hilarious effect uttered from someone in a cute T-shirt and capris.

"Holy shit!" Jessica gargled from the bathroom. Then: "Ohhhh, I shouldn't have had that fourth yogurt."

I never got sick of being the only one *not* to get something. "What? Are we still killing him? What's wrong? C'mon, break out the hand puppets, somebody. What? Whaaaaaaat?"

"My name *isn't* Nick," Nick told me. "It's Dick. I'm Nick in the other timeline. *Your original timeline.* I'm here, so I'm not here."

"Talking with you makes me feel like I'm rereading *Alice in Wonderland*." This was a lie. I'd never been able to make it through the book, and I thought the Johnny Depp movie was a little too pleased with itself.

"Which begs the question," Sinclair said. "Who are you, really? And why are you here, really?"

And why wouldn't Advil work on the undead, really? Someone should do a study. Unfortunately, I now had other things to worry about.

CHAPTER
FIFTEEN

"Wait, wait, wait. Wait." Everyone waited. *Unfortunately, that* was all I had. But wait! I had more. "So this Marc Thing, the dead guy in our kitchen right now, he's not in his past. He's in *our* past." I turned to him. "Is that right? You don't remember any of this?"

"I remember it," he said. "Just not this way."

I scowled. Maybe he could be *less* helpful. "So, no, then."

"What difference does it make?" Laura asked. "He's evil and he's gotta go."

"You are correct, but we need to talk about this for a bit," Sinclair said. "Murder is an irreversible action. I try to avoid irreversible actions when at all possible."

"Does this mean we can't fix the past? His past?" I asked,

pointing to the trussed vamp. "We're on . . . what? A parallel route now? Separate events and they can't ever touch in the way that parallel things can't ever touch, which I learned in sixth grade and never thought I'd have a use for?"

"Fifth grade!" Jessica called from the ralph room.

"The past already happened," the Marc Thing volunteered. "You can't un-happen something. Hrrmm. That came out more ignorant than I intended. And duller! What I meant was—"

"Wait!" I leaped to my feet . . . then remembered I'd already been standing and almost pitched into a wall. I was too excited to sit still. "I mean, wait again. We don't have to sit around and blah-blah this one to death."

"But I wanted to," Still Human Marc whined. "If I'm not in here, I've gotta go to work. I've mentioned it's a full moon, right? There'll be things to remove from rectums and lacerations to be stitched."

"No, this is a good thing! Don't you get it? I'll check the Book of the Dead! That's the whole reason I went to hell in the first place and let Laura beat me up for three centuries."

"You let Laura beat you up for three—"

"No time, Jess. Anyway, that's why I went through all that. So I could read the thing without going crazy. Finally, the stupid thing will actually come in handy instead of being awful and scary." I whirled and practically ran out of the kitchen.

"Wait," Laura began.

"What good is having an all-seeing creepy dead book of skin that's always right if I can't ever take advantage of it? Huh?" The hallway was narrow, so they were all stampeding behind me. Onward! I would lead my faithful minions to the path of the righteous, and also the library. "Right? Right? So I'll read it and it'll tell us what to do. Or at least what happened. *Then* we can make a plan. Then we can make another supper. Because I don't know about you guys, but I'm wicked thirsty."

"Betsy," Laura called again, but I was one heedless queen of the undead. It was so rare for me to get a really good idea, I couldn't wait to implement this one. I practically skidded to a halt in the library, which was harder than you'd think, what with the 1970s apricot shag. "Now we—shit."

"What?"

I pointed; the unholy book stand upon which the unholy and smelly Book of the Dead evilly perched was empty.

The book was gone. And thank goodness. Wow, was I glad the thing had gone missing. Now I didn't to worry about it, right? Because up until that point I had nooooo problems, right? And everything was working according to my plan, right?

Right. Gah.

CHAPTER
SIXTEEN

There was a long, perplexed silence, broken by N/Dick's, "Was it insured?"

"We're not putting in an insurance claim on the Book of the Dead," Jessica said firmly. "First off, we never got it appraised."

"Where is it?" I couldn't believe my eyes. I was at a total loss. Of all the problems I thought I'd have this month, releasing the hounds on a book bound in human skin was nowhere on the list. Don't even get me started on insurance paperwork.

"Okay, who was reading the Book of the Dead in the tub and forgot to put it back?" Marc asked, but if his expression was any indication, his heart wasn't in the teasing. He looked like I felt: rattled to the extreme.

"Wait." I turned to Tina and my husband. "There *is* a book in this timeline, right? You didn't follow me down the hallway to humor me? Or chase me?"

He smiled. "Though I will admit I have chased you from time to time, you are correct: there is a Book of the Dead in this timeline."

"Okay, that's something. So let's think about this for a minute. Did you know it was missing?"

"I took it."

"Of course not. I would have mentioned it straightaway." Sinclair looked as offended as I'd seen him. "After properly greeting you."

"Getting laid," N/Dick volunteered with a grin. He was recovering from the shattering blow quicker than the rest of us. Cops: they live in a black-and-white world. He didn't take it, he didn't know who did, he was waiting for instructions, then he'd get back in gear. Boom. Simple.

"As I said."

"I took it."

"Did *any* of you know it was missing?"

"You're asking *us*?" Marc said. "There's so much weird shit going on around here I don't even notice when my underwear's missing."

"Okay, first? Gross. And second, what now?"

"No one could have broken in here and taken it," Tina thought aloud. "Perhaps that other Marc secreted it somewhere before making his presence known?"

Dimly, from several rooms away: "I did not!"

"I took it."

"We gotta find it!" I was trying, and failing, not to freak out. What was worse than having the Book of the Dead in your house? Not knowing where the Book of the Dead was. I'd almost rather have a bitchy cobra roaming the carpets. "Whoever's reading it is reading it and going insane right this minute and maybe they don't even know it because they don't know when they read it they'll go insane! We have to save them!"

"Or punish them."

"Vengeful is not a good look for you," I told my husband. "Your nostrils get all flare-y."

"I took it."

"When did we last see it?" Tina asked. "If we can corroborate the last time it was here, we can then—"

"I took the Book of the Dead, you morons!"

We stared at the Antichrist. Nobody spoke for a few seconds, until the Marc Thing wailed, "Naaaaughty!"

CHAPTER
SEVENTEEN

"What?"

"I took it." Laura smoothed her bangs and tried not to look rattled. The library, which had always seemed dark and dusty to me, with the dark paneling and yucky apricot carpeting and dusty, dark, overstuffed furniture, seemed to loom, then shrink, around me.

Remember wishing there was a cobra on the loose? Now I felt like there really had been one, only she'd been with me the whole time.

"You what?"

"I took the book."

"But why? Did you need some light reading while waiting in line at *Goodwill*?"

"I took it after I got here."

Right. I remembered—after she realized the Marc Thing had followed us back, she put on a big show of being revolted and horrified. Or maybe she really had been revolted and horrified. Either way, she'd left the kitchen on the premise of making sure he hadn't left us any other surprises. Then . . . took the Book? But . . . "How come?"

She glanced at the carpet, the window, the sofa, her feet, my feet, my neck, and finally my face. "You don't need it."

"What?"

"Am I not speaking clearly?" she snapped. "Why are you having trouble following this?"

"Are you seriously asking me that, you Antichristing sneaky jerkoff asshat?" (I'll admit it: I was stressed out. It had been a terrible week. Or three centuries. Or future.)

"Ah . . . Majesty . . ."

"Elizabeth, perhaps cooler heads could—"

"You bop in from freakin' *Goodwill* and then steal the nastiest thing in the house, and don't *say* anything until we need it and have to look all *over* for it? Who *does* that?"

"You checked *one* room," Laura said. "Barely, I might add. You came, you glanced, you bitched."

I gargled with fresh rage. "After being all egging-on with the killing of the Marc Thing?" I had thought at the time it had been out of character for her, but didn't follow up. Also, stealing and lying? Also out of character.

From several rooms away: "I don't mind! Really!"

D-Nick/Jessica/Still Human Marc: "Shut up!"

"Have you lost your teeny tiny mind, you too-tall, too-skinny, too-crazy jerk?"

"Oh, look who's talking, Miss Let's Blunder Around the Time Stream and Hang the Consequences! Thanks to you, we've got a dead Marc and a live Marc in the same timeline . . . in the same house! Thanks to you, I got chomped on by a dim, blonde, undead, selfish, whorish, blood-sucking leech when I was minding my own business in the past."

"Don't you call me dim!"

"Um. Everyone. Perhaps we should——" Tina began.

"Wait, *when* did this happen?" Marc asked. He had the look of a man desperately trying to buy a vowel. "Past, an hour ago? Past, last year? Help me out."

"Oh, biiiiig surprise!" Laura threw her (perfectly manicured) hands in the air. "Let me guess, you were soooo busy banging your dead husband that you haven't had time to tell anybody anything."

"I was getting to it," I whined.

"Then after *not* telling anyone anything and *not* being proactive——or even active!——you grow up to destroy the world and bring about eternal nuclear winter or whatever

the heck *that* was and how do you deal with your foreknowl-
edge of terrible events to come? Have sex!"

"An affirmation of life?" Sinclair suggested. Never, I
repeat, never had I loved him more. I was torn between slug-
ging my sister and blowing my husband. Hmm. Laura might
have a point about my priorities . . . but jeez. *Look* at him.
Yum.

"—even do it and what do you have to say for yourself? Huh?"

"You're just uptight, repressed, smug, antisex, *and* jealous,
you Antichristing morally superior, fundamentally evil bitch."

Laura and Marc gasped. My husband groaned.

"That's right." I gripped the gold cross around my neck and wiggled it back and forth at her. I'd had to sling it all the way around so it was on my back when Sinclair and I were, um, busy earlier. Nothing kills the mood faster than a third-degree burn between the nipples. His, not mine.

Laura's color-of-a-spring-sky eyes were slits. "I am not *jealous.*"

"Wait, that's the word you're refuting?" Jessica asked. "Out of that whole thing she just said?"

"I'm trying to help you. I'm trying to keep you safe. And because you're you, you're blocking me all over the place."

My husband and friends had the look of people watching the most terrifying yet coolest tennis match in the history of human events. I didn't remember moving, but I was nose-to-nose with my little sister, shaking my (unmanicured . . . the older I got, the harder it was to find time to do vital stuff like nail maintenance) finger under her chin, and she wasn't backing down an inch.

"And in case you lost track of time in hell or at *Goodwill*, I've only been back about three hours! It's not like I went on a shopping spree without warning anybody." This time. "But never mind me, Miss Sneaky Pants. Let's get back to you, and how you're sneaky. You ducked out to hide the book, and I can't help notice you haven't." I lightly pushed her with tented fingers. "Given." Push. "It *back*."

"I already told you." She settled her stance so my fingers weren't rocking her back and forth. "You don't need it."

"Not. Your. Ennnff! Decision." Damn. She could really brace herself when she wanted.

"Ladies," Sinclair tried.

"To think I could be stitching up drunks and missing this!" Marc gurgled.

"Get her!" the Marc Thing yelled. I had no idea who he was rooting for.

"It's *mine*." I couldn't believe I was pissed because someone had grabbed the book I loathed and was keeping it from me so I couldn't read it to find out terrible things I could do nothing about.

Weirder: I couldn't believe I was pissed because I truly felt my property had been stolen! How could my life and death have gotten so fucked up in three years?

Come on, Betsy. Time to wake up. You're having a terrible dream because you missed the sweater sale at Saks, but things will be better once you wake up. Wake up! "So cough it up."

"Why do you even care? You hate it. Everybody knows you hate it . . . Lord knows you complain about it enough."

"What the Lord knows and keeps to Himself is none of your business. You know I hate it? So you just come in and snatch it? I hate famine and poverty, too, so what's your plan for those?"

"The important thing," Tina began, "is that it is no longer missing. And I am sure Laura will—"

"Back off," I snapped in unison with Laura's, "Stay out of this, you lesbian slut."

"Hey! Tina is a bisexual slut."

"Thank you, my queen," Tina murmured as N/Dick slowly shook his head and stared at the floor. I knew that look. He was afraid he was going to laugh, even as he knew baaaad shit could happen at any second.

"How do you not see how twisted and stupid this is, Laura? You know, you *know* the whole reason I went to hell was because your evil, evil, evil, evil mom promised me that if I did, I could read the fucking thing and not get a nine-day migraine or turn evil. So why take it now that I can finally read it?"

"I thought you went to hell so you could help me learn about my powers," Laura said sadly.

Okay. Whoa. That stopped me right there. I instantly felt like an unworthy shit. She just sounded so . . . dejected. I reminded myself she was just a kid—was she even drinking age yet? A lonely kid with the devil for a mom and powers she couldn't control—and a destiny she didn't want.

"Well, yeah. That, too. Don't get me wrong, I enjoyed our zany adventures." *Huge* lie. "And when your mom explained the best way for you to get in touch with your abilities was to smack me around? Hilarious!" Huger lie. "But you're forgetting something, Laura. Before we went anywhere, you called *me*, remember? *You* woke up naked in the spoon and called *me* for help."

"Waaaaait!" the Marc Thing wailed. "What are you talking about? What spooooon?"

"Then I ended up talking to your mom and making the deal. That's how all this started, right?" I softened my tone. "Well, we're back now, and we've got more work to do—you know, saving the world, and saving Marc—"

Marc smiled, pleased. "Thank you."

From the kitchen: "It won't work! You won't save him! We're dooooooomed. In every timeline, I think. So kill us both, Spock!" Psycho vamps channeling *Star Trek* . . . so this is what they meant by hell in a hand basket.

"That duct tape is working so great," Jessica whispered to Dickie/Nickie. "Why didn't we gag him with a roll of it?"

He shrugged, not taking his gaze off me. "Hindsight." It wasn't the first time I noticed Nick was standing almost entirely in front of Jessica. Protecting her, like. It looked so natural—practiced?—and Jess didn't even notice. In this timeline they were in love, he liked me and tolerated the shenanigans from House o' Vamps, but was also mindful of the danger. I liked him a lot for it.

"Betsy? What?"

I blinked and looked at Laura. Sinclair leaned in and muttered, "You were explaining that you needed each other and helped each other, but now have a new agenda."

"Yea, that. An agenda like you and me not getting evil, or more evil, so please give me back my Book of the Dead now so we can get on with whatever it is."

Wait. Had I really just phrased it like that?

"It's not *your* Book of the Dead," Laura pointed out.

"It follows me around like a dumb, ugly, smelly dog," I said, irritated. "Whose else would it be?"

"You don't need it and you shouldn't use it. I'll take it to hell and let you know what you're supposed to know."

"What, because you're the Antichrist you won't go crazy

if you read it? Or is your devil mom going to translate for you?"

"Either way, Laura, as my queen rightly pointed out, that is not your decision," Sinclair said. You could practically hear the icicles in his voice. "She requires her property. I require your obedience to my queen."

"Well, why not?"

"Why not, *what?*" I nearly screamed. How long had we been having this argument? Eight months? Gah.

"Why isn't it my decision? I'm more powerful than you are, and I can call on my mom if we need help. I should hang on to the book. Right?"

"Right? *Right?* No, that's not *right.* It stayed with Sinclair until I became a vampire, then it stayed with me. It never had anything to do with you, but now you've decided you should have it? And you're all mystified because I'm pissed?"

"You're always pissed," my little sister mumbled, and I could have happily slapped her perfect complexion. "Should have done it a long time ago anyway."

I swayed in my shoes. Words. They really failed me. *You sneaky cow! Did you lose a bet?* Nope, nope. *How long have you been a slobbering sociopath?* Nuh-uh, not quite right.

"Will you cut the shit already?" That was better, but still not great. "What's wrong with you, you loon?"

"It's just that some things, you don't need to know and

you shouldn't know. Just because you can check on the future doesn't mean you should. You need to stay as far away as you can from that book."

"Oh, barf. You're majoring in Sneaky, which is just so lame! You pretend to rush over to help me, on the way to *Goodwill* no less . . ." For some reason I couldn't let that one go. It really bugged me. "Because that's your thing, you do these showy goody-goody things like teaching Sunday school and giving clothes to the poor while at the same time you're smacking me to time travel, admiring your weird wings in hell, *not* telling your mother to butt out of your life, sneaking around my house, stealing books bound in skin, not saying anything, *not* giving it back, and pretending it's because *I'm* the bad guy? You know what, Laura?"

"Don't say it," Laura cautioned.

"Majesty—"

"My queen—" Sinclair looked distinctly constipated. I could tell he wanted to clap his hand over my mouth, but didn't quite dare. "Please—"

"You are—"

"You better not," the Antichrist warned.

"You are your *mother's daughter*!"

From down the hall: "Oh no she dih-unt!"

The room shot to the side. This was amazing and scary—then I realized Laura had clocked me on the chin with her tiny fist of evil. Before Sinclair or Tina or anyone could do anything, I saw a sight that had become waaaay too familiar in the last few days/centuries: a portal into hell had opened right there in our library, courtesy of the Antichrist striking her flesh-and-blood in anger.

It led to hell; the doorway was made of Hellfire, and yes, I'm aware of how high that description hits on the Lame-O-Meter. But it was the best I could do—the doorway-sized entrance glowed with a sort of dark fire. Tina and Sinclair had both ducked behind their raised forearms and I remembered that Hellfire was lethal to vampires.

Except me. Along with the crown and the studly husband, I got eternal immunity from holy water, crosses, Hellfire, and laugh lines. And blisters and corns.

"I'm leaving," my sister told me, "before we say things we regret."

"How's that even possible?" I wondered. "You'd really have to put some time in to figure out how you could say things that are more regretful." Then, "No you don't!"

I reached out and blindly grabbed. Laura yelped as I jerked her head back—I had a double fistful of Suave-scented golden tresses. She responded by kicking out, hard.

Snarling and scratching and pulling, we fell into hell.

CHAPTER
NINETEEN

It's hard to describe what happened next—it was fast, and it was dirty and weird. Not dear-*Penthouse*-forum-you-won't-believe-what-happened-to-me-last-Groundhog-Day dirty and weird, either. The bad dirty and weird.

We fell. We fell for a long time, or maybe just half a second, we were pulling a Gandalf and we fell somewhere while Hellfire whipped past us and even *through* us (don't ask me; no clue). We fell, and I could hear whooshing and shouting and sounds I didn't in the least understand, sounds I had never heard in my life, sounds I never wanted to hear again.

My head hurt from Laura's flurry of punches, my toes hurt from kicking her shins. I wished the Antichrist were a guy so I could rack him in the balls. I wished I were still holed up in our bedroom with Sinclair. I wished I were wearing my Jimmy Choo snake-embossed pumps . . . the toes came to a wicked point. I wished I hadn't had that extra smoothie . . . it was possible I was going to be the first vampire queen to barf strawberry smoothie all over a portal to/through hell. Urrgg . . . make that a strawberry-banana smoothie . . .

"Get . . . *off*!" my sister shrieked, and managed to wrench herself free. This would be a shameful, shameful thing except we were in hell, her territory. And I was scared.

Not of her—okay, a little of her. I'd seen a side of Laura today I'd never dreamed existed. Which made me a moron, since I'd seen her kill people.

But I was too new to being a vampire . . . I was afraid if I really fought back I'd hurt her in a way someone who was half fallen angel couldn't get back from. She might be the badass Antichrist, but she had a human body, which came with a skull and a neck, and both were breakable. So I let her twist free.

Which was dumb, in retrospect. I fell again (still?). Except this time, I didn't have a guide cursing me as we plummeted.

Wake up.

I didn't have anyone.

Wake up, Betsy!

I just kept falling, alone.

Wake up!

Forever. Or maybe it was only for half a second. Falling through hell, and me without a watch.

At the precise moment the whooshing eerie warblings of hell
cut out, the familiar sounds of big-city traffic cut in. And
it wasn't gradual, like clicking the volume with the remote
until it got as loud as you like, while at the same time too
loud as far as your mother's concerned.

No, it was *whoosh/crash/bang.* I realized I was on my hands
and knees in . . . a city street? Yes. A city street. A busy
city street. Okay, great. Not falling, and not in hell anymore. Things could be worse. Things *had* been worse.

I shakily stood and was relieved to hear another familiar
sound: the shriek of stomped-on brakes.

Wait, brakes? Stomped-on brakes?

Hey, I can fly! A new superpower; this vampire thing was getting cooler all the time. Check me out!

And I could fly *fast.* I shot by all sorts of shiny surfaces—man, I looked cool! Like Supergirl, except with a better rack.

"Look at meeeee, the vampire queeeen, so pretty, so rare, with the wind in her hair—"

(Ow.)

TWENTY-ONE

And that's how I ended up in the Cook County Morgue. In friggin' *Chicago.* Who knew there was a portal from my St. Paul house to hell to The Magnificent Mile in Chicago? Not that it seemed so magnificent when the fish truck creamed me and knocked me through a (meditate on the irony) Payless Shoes store window.

Of course they thought I was dead and stuffed me into a smelly body bag. You know how when you get new inflatable toys for summer swimming and they have that peculiar plastic-ey smell? Yup, like that. Except a dark color so blood and other fluids wouldn't show up. Oh, and the zipper. Let's not forget the great big zipper.

Screeeeech, kee-RASH! Thump, thud. Broken glass everywhere.

Pulseless (yet sexy) corpse buried under dozens of buy-one-get-the-second-half-off anklet boots in many unflattering dark colors. It was like being buried under a mountain of Splenda when you wanted real sugar. Or being trapped in a cave with nothing but diet pop when you wanted the real deal.

Sing it with me: "Weeeeee're *off* to see the coroner, the wonderful, wonderful coroner. We hear he is a whiz with a knife, if ever a whiz there was! If ever a knife could cut up my type, could cut up my type and make me feel right, we—" Never mind. That sucked. And when did I start making up songs in my head?

I had to put the whammy on the poor guy who had been paid by the county to cut me open and weigh my internal organs. Don't judge: I normally tried to feed only on the jerky, or my husband. But these were dire times. I had to get back to St. Paul. I had to find Laura. I had to find some underpants.

I didn't know where my old clothes were, and didn't care. They were probably all bloody and ruined, anyway, bagged and tagged and sitting in another cold room. It's not like I'd been carrying ID; anything that identified me was still in St. Paul. Anyway, who'd connect an unsatisfied dead morgue customer in Chicago to weird goings-on in St. Paul?

That said, I wasn't going to be naked for another minute.

I was able to scrounge, with the help of my newest fan, the dazed and bitten Dr. Graham, clean scrub pants in poop brown, a "Stereotypes Are a Real Time-saver" T-shirt a size too small, but not in a sexy way, and bare feet.

Bare feet! In November! No problem; it was either that or paper slippers. Or Dr. Graham's shower slippers, little rubber boats of fungus. I nearly screamed when he tried to hand them to me. We were both having a shitty day.

"I'd say something like 'this is hell,'" I told the goofily smiling Dr. Graham, "except I've been to hell and this is worse." At my gesture, he handed over his cell phone. "Thanks. Uh, some privacy, please?"

Graham wandered off, holding his neck. I stabbed a phone number that was practically tattooed on my heart, the private cell number of my beloved . . .

"Elizabeth? Hello?"

. . . a number only two people on the entire planet knew, we each had the other's soul and we each had the other's private cell number . . .

"Elizabeth? Are you hurt?"

. . . because that's how special I was to him. That's how special his cell number was to me. Also his Bergdorf discount. It was comforting to know that in a world gone wild, and a hell gone worse—

"Elizabeth!"

"Ow, don't *scream*. Shrill is not a good sound for you."

"Ohthankwhoeveryou'reallright," he gasped. It was kind of funny . . . Sinclair wanted to thank God, except if he said the actual word, he'd probably get blisters in his mouth.

"That's okay," I said. "I'll thank Him for you. I pray for you every night anyway. Well, almost every night. Okay, every week. What is this, a witch hunt? Once a month for sure."

"WHERE THE HELL ARE YOU?"

"Oh, you can just take that tone and jam it right up into your teal blue silk boxers from ManSilks, pal! You have no idea of the hell I've been through. Literally. It's wrong that I know that. *No one should know that!*"

"I am going to lock you in a room and fuck you for hours," the king of the vampires growled, "and then I will kill you. Where are you?"

That sounded pretty good. The first part.

"Elizabeth!"

"I'm in a Roadrunner cartoon, Sinclair. And I'm the coyote." The events of the last few hours/centuries got on top of me at that moment and I burst into tears. "Come get me, Sinclair, okay? Sinclair? Okay?" I was crying harder and couldn't hear him, but *could* hear how pathetic I sounded, so I hung up.

I slid down the wall; Dr. Graham had kindly escorted me to a different part of the basement and I had privacy for my meltdown. So I sobbed and stretched out my legs and kicked my bare feet and slapped the wall and wiped my eyes with the cell—I couldn't make tears, but old habits, you know?— and it beeped in my hand.

"Who is it?" I wept. "Dr. Graham isn't here. And I shouldn't be."

"My own, my queen, you forgot to tell me where you are."

I cried harder. "Sorry. I'm having a terrible night."

"Don't cry, Elizabeth, it tears my heart."

"And I don't have any shoes!"

"And yet you must find the strength to go on," the king of the vampires soothed.

"Are you making fun of me?"

"Never. And I would instantly destroy the soulless cur who would dare."

"Yeah, that would be good. Destroying soulless curs." I perked up a little. "Okay. I love you."

"I love you to, my own, but—"

"Here comes Dr. Graham. I better—"

"Elizabeth!"

"Don't *yell*, I'm having a bad night!"

"Where. The hell. Are you. My love?"

"Oh. Yeah, that would be helpful, wouldn't it? Chicago. Cook County Morgue."

A long sigh on the other end, which was cute since Sinclair

didn't have to breathe. He sometimes forgot when he was aggravated.

"We are coming, my own. I will see you in less than six hours."

"Six hours? It's dark now; what's the holdup? What about Jessica's private pl—?"

"If anyone gets between thee and me, I want you to kill them, Elizabeth. Even . . ."

"Even what?"

"Even if they are friends."

"Yeah, I'm gonna take a pass on that."

"Or were friends. You are far from me, darling, and many of our people have not yet accepted you as queen. The city of Chicago should not know the vampire queen is there, alone. Stay low if you can. Find a sheep if you can, and hole up with him or her and get your strength back."

"Sinclair!" I was truly shocked. People weren't *sheep*. What I had done to Dr. Graham was bad enough; I wasn't going to haul some pour soul off the street, make them take me to their home, then feed on them like a blond wood tick 'til the cavalry came while I emptied their fridge of all things liquid. Guh-ross!

He sighed again. "If you cannot or will not take such measures, protect yourself however you can. And, Elizabeth . . ."

"Yeah?" I'd gone from comforted to scared and lonely.

"Don't pray for me. Pray for you. And tell . . . tell Him"—
his voice was getting choked, difficult to hear—". . . to . . .
to keep you safe."

"I will," I said, touched. "I love you."

"Yes," he said, and clicked off, the arrogant ass.

TWENTY-TWO

Hours later, the good Dr. Graham's phone beeped again. Tina this time, with curt directions. Not even so much as a "thank goodness you're safe, Your Majesty." I swear, she could have out-Pattoned Patton.

I promised obedience, then thanked Dr. Graham and gave him back his phone. When I asked if he was going to get into trouble, he laughed even as he erased everything on his phone. I hadn't told him to do that, and Tina hadn't told me to tell him to do that . . . *that* was interesting. He was either good at precautions or a coward. Or both.

"Bodies go missing here all the time. Actual dead ones, not bodies like yours, not ones that get up and walk around."

He was staring at my tits. He'd had a bad night, so I didn't smack him. Stupid too-small T-shirt.

"I could probably make you forget everything that happened," I suggested. "Then you wouldn't be scared or horny or both. You'd just be . . . however you are when you haven't been attacked by a ruthless naked denizen of the undead."

"Don't you dare." He held up his hands and backed away. "You keep your vampire hypnosis to yourself. I earned those memories; you can't have them."

"Okay, okay, simmer. Sorry again. You better go, my ride's here."

"Yeah, and I have to go drink a whole bunch of vodka . . . for a long, long time . . . nice to meet you, I guess . . ." Graham wandered away, and I went out to the loading area Tina had told me about (thank goodness for the Internet).

Unloading area, actually—I was standing (blurgh!) where they dropped off the dead bodies. The ones that were better at staying dead than I was. I don't know how Tina managed it, either, but the unloading area was empty. It was like a big creepy warehouse, very well lit (the fortune they must spend on gigantic fluorescent bulbs!) and clean. It was just me, and all the lights, and my ride.

And what a ride!

CHAPTER TWENTY-THREE

"Whoa." I had seen many strange things in the last three years, including my own tombstone ("Our Sweetheart, Only Resting" . . . barf), but nothing came close to this.

The largest and most luxurious RV I had ever seen was majestically rolling into the (un)loading area. It was cream with brown trim, and the windows all looked shiny clean and six feet high. Then the doors underneath—where, if it were a Greyhound bus, all the luggage would be stored— the doors underneath smoothly rolled up revealing . . . a red two-seater Ferrari. Sinclair's Ferrari!

"What the—"

The front door to the RV burst open and I half expected a

dozen clowns to pour out. But Tina was framed in the doorway. She'd changed into white leggings (show-off bitch . . . if I'd tried white leggings my thighs would look like Christmas hams) and a sky blue turtleneck. She looked like a ski bunny. Who could kill you and eat you and hide the body where no one would ever, ever find it. "My queen! I'm so relieved you're safe!"

Then, in an unprecedented act, she was shoved aside and skinned her nose on the pavement as Sinclair galloped joyfully toward me. He hugged me so hard he knocked me off my feet. I knew Tina, being solicitously helped off the pavement by Marc, would forgive her king's unchivalrous action—she looked positively delighted to have scraped knees and palms and nose, which rapidly healed even as I stared.

"I'm happy to nnngggg—" I've mentioned I didn't need much oxygen, right? And it was a good thing, too. Sinclair was busily smooshing my poor lungs into undead airless lumps in the center of my chest. "Ooooommmmggggggrrrrggglll . . . ack!"

"My love, my love, I am so grateful you are safe." Sinclair said all this into my neck and I felt a sharp pain as he bit me.

That was rare—my husband was normally the epitome of control and only showed his teeth in the bedroom. Or to random rapists. (It was wrong that I liked being rapist

bait and then my hubby and I both fed on said bait, right?)
That uncontrolled bite told me everything I needed to know
about his worry, and his love.

"Aw, come on," I said.

"Never scare me like that again. Never never never."

"You're too lame and uptight to be a widower, though no
worrieth." Oh, dammit. The smell of my own blood, the heat
of our excitement, had made my fangs pop, too. Stupid vampire lisp.

Sinclair laughed into my neck, a deep, joy-filled bellow.
Then he was dragging me past Marc and Tina—

"Hey, guys, thanks for—"

"Whoops, there they go, off to compete yet again in the
Sexual Olympics." Marc shook his head. "New record."

—and up the steps of the super RV, past Nick, who was
waving at us from the wheel—

"—riding to my rescue—"

—past the gorgeous furniture and accessories, this thing
was a *mansion* on eight wheels! Or twelve . . . How many
did RVs have?

"—and picking me up!" I hollered before we were in the
bedroom and Sinclair kicked the door closed. Which was
fine with me. If you were wondering.

TWENTY-FOUR

You'd think we hadn't had fast nasty sex earlier that day. Or the morning before—I had no idea what time it was, which day of the week it was, how long I'd been back from hell, how long it had been since I got run over on The Magnificent (ha!) Mile, what hideous terrible thing we had to avert, who was alive in this timeline, who was dead, and who we had to save, nor did I care.

My husband demonstrated his pleasure in our reunion by shredding my borrowed shirt, ripping my borrowed scrubs off, yanking his own shirt off, nearly strangling himself by removing his tie (who wears a tie on a rescue mission?), and though he managed to get his belt unbuckled and his fly down, he couldn't quite manage to rid himself of his slacks before he fell on me.

Which was fine by me; I was the ultimate welcoming vessel. I practically had a "Help Yourself, Neighbor!" sign hung around my neck. Our mouths nearly slammed together, his teeth cut me, hurt me, and I didn't give a ripe shit.

He seized my thighs and slung them apart, then surged forward and I felt his cock enter between my thighs and stop somewhere around my throat. Felt his mouth on my neck, nuzzling, not biting, and heard him, heard him murmuring into my throat, "Sorry, sorry, my own, my queen, oh forgive . . . oh . . . oh . . ."

He . . . he thought he was hurting me! Which he was. But, as above: I didn't give a ripe shit. I loved it; I loved *him*. It didn't matter what he did to me; I'd heal in minutes or even seconds. It was worth anything. It was worth anything to be with him.

I had to die to learn about love.

Dumbass.

(*Love I love I love O Elizabeth I love I love . . .*)

(*Don't stop. If you stop, I'm getting a divorce lawyer.*)

(*Love O I love O O O O O O O O O O O O O!*)

I saw stars. Cliché, right? But they were streaming past

my eyes, they were screaming through my heart. They were everywhere, *we* were everywhere, and while we were together it was impossible to worry, or be scared, or . . .

. . . or anything.

CHAPTER TWENTY-FIVE

"Are you . . . all right?"

"Extremely very all right." I scratched at some of the dried blood, which had pooled in the center of my throat. "Aw. You were worried."

"I think I shall kill you soon," he speculated to the ceiling. "After I use your body more, of course."

"Of course. Wouldn't have it any other way. Not a jury in the world would convict you."

He didn't laugh, or even smile. His hand, which had been gently cradling my wrist, tightened. "I was . . . afraid."

"Me, too. I do not like being run over on the so-called Magnificent Mile. And I'm going to wring Laura's neck when we see her."

"Yes." I didn't think I'd ever heard him sound so grim, so I tried to cheer him up.

"But you're here now. And we'll figure it all out."

He turned and was looming over me, his dark eyes piercing, his forehead furrowed. He looked terribly, terribly concerned. "What? What will we figure out?"

"What we have to. Sinclair, don't you know? Didn't you read the memo? We can do anything. Anything."

"I love you," he said, and kissed me deeply. His mouth tasted mine for a long, long time and I remembered, again, that I had to die to understand about love.

I broke the kiss, and not without regret.

"Something I've always wondered, Sinclair. And by 'always' I mean 'for the last few hours.'"

"Ah, I await all a-tremble for your random comment."

"If you died when you were in your late teens, why do you look like a handsome-but-weathered thirty? I can remember first meeting you and thinking you were thirtysomething, but in the past you were just a kid. Younger than Laura, even! Oooh, don't get me started on Laura."

"I shall not, then." My husband wiggled his dark brows at me. Like me, and Jim Carrey, he had the gene that let him raise them independently. He hardly ever indulged, so it was hilarious when he did. Over the sound of my appreciative snort, he said, "You recall, of course, that my last week of life as a human being was somewhat stress-ful."

"Dead sister, dead parents." My throat tightened. How would I handle it if my mom . . . if BabyJon . . . bad enough to contemplate the scenario at all, but to lose them both the same *week*?

Leaving Eric Sinclair alone . . . with Tina, his family's very own pet vampire. Small wonder he made the decision he had. And it worked. And it was a bargain. The only price he paid was his soul . . . and decades of loneliness.

My father and stepmother's deaths were startling, but not all that traumatic. Hey, I'm not going to pretend I loved her. I mean them. We never got along; death didn't change that. Or her. I mean them.

"That's just . . . I don't have the words."

"A rare and wondrous occasion."

"And I'm so sorry. I was sorry then and I haven't—I didn't have a chance to tell you—I guess I should tell you now. I'm so, so sorry."

"I know," he said, and leaned in and kissed me above my left eyebrow. "I know the things you think, and cannot say."

"Okay, creepy. But we'll get to that another time. But about your past—about your sister and—and—I can't believe you didn't jump off a bridge."

His eyebrows climbed higher, if that was possible. "In a

manner of speaking, I did. Certainly I was dead quite soon after. But even if I hadn't endured the worst week of my life, it was the early twentieth century, darling. We lived hard."

"And ate hard. I can still taste your delicious live blood. I can't believe I just said that."

"Speaking of your bite, beloved . . ."

"Were we?"

He was licking the column of my throat. "Not . . . precisely . . ."

"Wow!"

"Really?" He looked pleased, and licked harder.

"This is the coolest room!"

He snorted, then rolled over so he was again on his back. "I had hopes I was dazzling you with my seductive skills."

I held up a double handful of shredded T-shirt and raised my eyebrows at him. The bum didn't even look apologetic, just pointed to some dresser drawers and went back to lolling. What is it about tearing clothing that made men all "me Tarzan" as opposed to embarrassed they showed the patience of a four-year-old?

The RV bedroom could have been an expensive Miami hotel room . . . everything was cream and chrome and glass. The carpet was *so* plush! The sofa was also cream, and beautiful . . . this was *not* a low-rent mobile home on wheels. Nor was it child-friendly. Plasma TV, mirrors everywhere. The living area, which I'd gotten a bare glimpse of while Sinclair was dragging me through it, was just as plush. Velvety cream-colored couches, small exquisite tables, swivel chairs, another TV . . . wow.

"It's not Jessica's private plane," I said, digging through the drawers, which someone (Tina . . . the clothes were appropriate and neatly folded) had stuffed full of my outfits. "But I suppose I can put up with the crudeness of a seven-figure recreational vehicle."

"Plane?"

"Mmmm." I jerked a thumb toward a door I assumed led to the bathroom. "Shower?"

"Of course." Sinclair bounded up from the bed like a big cat.

"I don't need a tour," I said, amused. Damn, he was a fine specimen of a man. Even if he was practically tripping because his slacks had clung to his ankles. I'd never seen a sexy stagger before.

"I wasn't going to give you a *tour*," he said, and I laughed.

I heard a lively honk and poked my fingers through the shades, making a tiny tent of the blinds. There, in the lane beside the Mansion on Wheels, were Tina and Marc . . . and Marc was driving Sinclair's Ferrari!

"I specifically told Marc he could *not*," Sinclair humphed, glaring out the window. Marc tooted more and zigged back and forth in the lane, waving. Tina was covering her eyes and shaking her head. "If we did not require a discreet physician who would never betray us . . ."

I was dazzled. This was the coolest week ever! Maybe. "Why'd you bring the monster RV *and* a car?"

"Oh, some silly nonsense they were bleating about not wanting to listen to our lovemaking."

"Nick must have lost the coin toss," I said, remembering I'd seen him at the wheel for half a second when I was hauled ("Thar she be, matey!") aboard the vessel like booty. Or booty (get it?).

"And quite cross about it, too," Sinclair said, and I laughed so hard I fell down.

That was okay, though. My husband kissed my boo-boos in the shower. Do I have to tell you it was shiny and luxurious and stuffed with high-end gels and shampoos?

CHAPTER TWENTY-SIX

"Well, finally," was how Jessica chose to greet me. Nice.
"I've been waiting all night. Literally all night. The sun's coming up pretty soon."

I was in no mood for discussing the hours I'd been in transit, or dead. "If you'd come with, you wouldn't have had to wait," I sniffed back. I was in zero mood for attitude. Too bad, because Jess had a belly full of it.

Tina and Sinclair had their heads together in one of the parlors, Marc was out parking the Ferrari in the garage, and Nick was getting the RV gassed again. I'd run right into the house to change my clothes and update my footgear. Tina had been a dear, but who packs flats with everything? *Everything?*

"Could have come with? Are you kidding me? A six-hour drive and me eight months pregnant? And knowing you and the King of Dick, you were banging all the way back to St. Paul, and there's only one bathroom in the Mystery Machine."

"Lame," I announced, though I was giggling. "Was your plane in the shop?"

"Plane?"

"Your private—you don't have a private plane in this timeline, do you?"

"In *this* economy?" Jessica looked horrified.

"Okay, that makes sense, but the private plane was cool. Though the Mystery Machine was an acceptable substitute. And Nick—"

"I knew," my (ugh!) stepmother announced from behind Jessica, "she'd be as big as a house when she got pregnant out of wedlock. Didn't I tell you?"

"Oh, yuck!"

"Don't be like that," Jessica said. "You don't have to be a jerk *all* the time."

"You're one to talk," I snapped back to the Ant. I wasn't going to make a fool of myself the way I did when I found out Garrett was alive. Betsy Taylor learns from her mistakes. Of all the people, though! Mother Teresa was dead and the Ant was alive?

"Mother Teresa's dead, right?" I whispered to Jessica.

"It's disgusting," my annoyingly alive stepmother continued. She was the only person I knew who could skulk as well as she mocked. "Flaunting that belly when she should be flaunting a wedding ring. And that sweater is too small. And all wrong for her complexion, which is too dark."

"You got knocked up to get married!" I cried, amazed, as always, at the Ant's selective memory.

"I did not!" Jess and the Ant said in unison.

"And your complexion's fine."

Jess blinked. "What?"

"Disgusting," the Ant said. She was everything a man could want: her hair was too dyed and too tall, her electric faux silk dress was too faux, her panty hose was all wrong for open-toed sandals, her faux fingernails were too red, she wasn't especially smart, she wasn't especially nice, and she used sex to get what she wanted.

Not in a romantic hey-Sinclair-let's-stay-in-bed-all-night-and-find-new-ways-to-hurt-each-other way. In a darling-let's-leave-your-seventh-grade-daughter-behind-when-we-go-on-vacation-so-we-can-make-Disney-World-just-for-the-two-of-us way.

Now, which one of her odious personality traits was I forgetting? Oh, yeah. She was a bigot, *and* a snob.

"Not you," I clarified, irritated. "*You.* What do you want, anyway? Shouldn't you be off in your too-expensive, too-big house neglecting your son BabyJon, the sweetest baby God ever made, whom you do *not* deserve? Or making my poor idiot of a father's life a living hell? And speaking of hell, your rotten daughter made the top of my shit list tonight, so I'll be bouncing her skull off the fireplace bricks for a while."

"Don't you touch her!" the Ant snapped. "She's more powerful than you'll ever be, and prettier."

"Liar!" I screamed. That was just—oooooh, low blow. Taller, maybe. I'd be okay with taller, maybe.

"Betsy!" Jessica screamed back. Oh, shit. Was labor rearing its ugly head? This was too much to ask of anyone, but especially me.

"Now look what you did," I snarled in the Ant's direction. "You've made her water blow up, or something."

"Betsy." Jessica's color-of-green-Play-Doh fingernails sunk into my wrist and I yelped. "Who are you talking to?"

"What the hell does that—" I pointed at the Ant, who was checking her shoulder pads for dandruff. "It. Her. That. Ish! Don't stare too long, you'll go blind. My stepmaggot. Antonia. Nice try, but pretending she's not there never works."

"Antonia's dead, Betsy."

"Moron," my dead stepmother added.

TWENTY-SEVEN

I greeted this news with a cheated roar: "Nobody tells me anything!"

"We thought you knew. You, uh, knew in the old time-line. So she's alive in—"

"Ick, no, they're both dead and I'm BabyJon's legal guardian."

"My poor boy," my dead stepmother mourned.

"You shut up from your corner of the damned. I just—I mean, I saw her there and . . ." It was too embarrassing to confess. No one could understand my unique shame.

"After you freaked out about Garrett being alive in front of the whole house," Jessica the Annoying speculated, "you assumed the Ant was alive and didn't want to make a total jackass of yourself again."

"How much do I hate thee?" I asked aloud. "Let me count the ways." Friends: the ultimate mixed blessing.

"Well, she is. And drives you crazier, if possible, in death than in life. She's saying something racist right now, isn't she?"

"She should wear prints so when she cleans houses, the dirt won't show up so badly."

"She says you've never looked prettier," I replied.

"Tell her I think she's a useless whore."

"She can see *you*. *She* doesn't need a translator. So she and my dad . . ."

"Oh, yeah."

"In a car vs. garbage truck accident?"

Jessica bit her lip so as not to smirk, and nodded. She had always been polite to the Ant, even in death.

"My life passed before my eyes," the Ant fretted, "and you were in a horrible amount of it."

"Are you Satan's receptionist in this timeline, too?" I demanded. "Because I need to talk to your treacherous kid, pronto. And maybe her mom. Her other mom."

"You leave her alone," the Ant warned. "You've got plenty enough to worry about without bothering my boss or my little girl."

"What's that supposed to—dammit!"

"She's vanished in an evil puff of Aqua Net, hasn't she?"

"The bad guys only stay around long enough to be unhelpful," I bitched. It was true! They randomly popped in and out of my life like Girl Scouts during cookie season. Except you could usually predict when Girl Scouts will show up hawking Thin Mints. "Then, poof."

CHAPTER TWENTY-EIGHT

I would definitely keep Big Fat Jessica around, despite the annoyance of The Belly. Not many women could tolerate vampires, their boyfriend's road trips to morgues, switching timelines, ghostly visits from dead bigots, and mysterious disappearances from same. "That's exactly what my boyfriend says, except about arsonists."

"Speaking of him—he brought the Mystery Machine to the morgue, and Nick did all the driving! There *and* back." I hated driving, so found this impressive. It's soooo boring. And just when you get going, some asshat Statie pulls you over. Like there aren't any murders and rapes going on, so they can nap under bridges and set speed traps for unwary vampires. Weak.

"Dick. Remember? He's Dick."

"I know, I was just testing you. Also, don't worry that he's not here. He had to go—"

"I know, he texted me." She waved her cell phone at me, then grinned at my scowl. "Don't start with the text bitching."

"Why is it suddenly uncool to spell? That's all I want to know." Just thinking about how texting had taken over *both* timelines was pissing me off. I stomped through our musty hallway—we had three housekeepers, but the mansion had been born before Lincoln, and there was always dust somewhere. "I wouldn't trust Dead Ant to tell the truth about this, but has my psycho traitor jerkweed asshat sister been by? Because I'm scratching her eyes out the next time I see her. Then I'm really going to go to work on her."

"No, we've just been massively worried about you since she yanked you into hell. No one's had time to even look for her—not that we could find a teleporter."

"Right." That's what she was now, wasn't she? Terrific. "It was terrible," I agreed. "You were right to fret. I've been run over by an Aztek and knocked through a Payless store window in the last three years. And felt up by a strange doctor!"

I must have slowed down, or she sped up, because I felt her big stomach whack into my back. It was surprisingly solid, which, for some reason, put me in a fouler mood. And also scared me. Why was it like a boulder? Shouldn't it be soft? Pregnancy was weird.

"If you've got that telepathic link with Sinclair," she huffed, trying to keep pace, "why did we have to wait until you stole a cell phone? After, uh, you got felt up by a strange doctor?"

My back actually itched where The Gut had smacked me. "Telepathy's great if we're having sex face-to-face. I mean, having sex. But multiple states away it's less reliable." In fact, I was still sort of amazed that I'd been able to hear Sinclair from two states away. I guess major stress had amped up our . . . what? Receiving abilities? I didn't know. There was so much about this bullshit vampire gig that I didn't understand, and maybe never would.

Not that my sex-pathy was any of her business. She was my best friend, but there were limits. Sex-pathy forever, telling Jess all the perv details, never.

"What is your problem?" Jessica demanded flatly.

"Oh, me? Hmm? Nothing much. I'm just a little busy juggling screwed timelines, looking out for the Antichrist, breaking out of morgues, and trying not to destroy the world with eternal winter."

"With *me*. What's your problem with me? Specifically"— she pointed to her enormous bulge—"this part of me?"

"I've got more important things to worry about than

143

what you're gestating," I lied, scratching my lower back, which itched madly. What if she had a baby *and* some sort of fungus going on under there?

"Not right now you don't." For a second she was almost as intimidating as Satan. Satan! "If you expect to leave this hallway under your own power, you'll own your shit."

"Own my . . . ? Okay, first, I don't even know what that means. Second . . ." Would I? Could I, even? I *did* love the front-heavy tart, even if she got pregnant in front of me behind my back. Oh, the hell with it. "Second, I'm jealous, okay?"

"Of Dickie?"

"Who? Oh. Nick. No, no. In fact, he's a delight in this timeline. You have no idea . . . the father of your demon-spawn was a real prick in the old timeline. Jealous, moody, shrill . . ." Like me, actually. But this was no time for self-introspection. "No, I'm jealous of *that*." I pointed to her bulge again.

Jessica looked down at it (as if she could look anywhere else), then back up at me. Bewilderment was written across her face; anyone (even me) could have seen how startled she was. "What? Why?"

"Why?" I cried. "Are you serious? Why would I be jealous? Why *wouldn't* I? In *your* timeline, in the last few months *you* remember, I had ages to get used to Nick-who-is-now-

Dick never being a jerk and you being a mom-to-be. Here, I've had about fourteen hours. Several of which, I might add, I was unconscious on a coroner's slab!"

"But what does that have to do with—"

"I'm used to being number one in your life, okay?"

"But—"

"Listen: in the old timeline, the one you can't remember, bad things happened to Nick—"

"Dick."

"No, he was Nick then. And bad things happened to him, things that were my fault. And it changed him, made him a different man than the one you repeatedly knocked boots with in disgusting and fertile ways. And so, in that other timeline where you knew what birth control pills were, he made you choose: him, or me. You chose me. That's the past I remember. In my head, that's how things are.

"Except they aren't! And I'm having a tough time handling it, okay? It's shitty and it's selfish, and it's also the truth, right? I liked being first with you. I liked that you picked me over him. Lame, right? Right."

"You're not actually letting me answer any of your questions," she tried.

"But that didn't happen here. You've got N/Dick here, and he has you, and when you have a baby it'll be all 'baby makes three' and you'll love it more than me."

"That's idiotic."

"Nuh-uh! It's a biological imperative. It's gonna happen. You won't have any choice. You'll *have* to love it. And feed and house it, and open a college fund for it, and take tons of pictures of it to bore other people with, and put it on the phone before it can even talk, which we'll all hate but pretend we don't . . . it's all this huge biological rule you'll have to follow."

Jessica's mouth twitched. "I meant, it's idiotic to be jealous of a baby who isn't even here yet."

"Think I don't know? It's also lame and beneath me." I paused and thought that over for a second. "Okay, not much is beneath me, come to think of it, so that last bit might not be true. But all the rest *is*. Look, like I said, I know it's selfish. But I can't help it. I don't like sharing you. Why am I obsessing about this when I have to save Marc and the future and also beat up my sister and remember the Ant is dead and get the other Antonia and get the book back?" I wondered aloud. Even for me, this was scattered. "Ugh, I hate everything tonight."

"Betsy . . ." Jessica seemed startled, almost flabbergasted. "I could have twins in here—"

"Don't you threaten me!"

Her eyes actually watered with the effort to not laugh in my face. "Triplets, even. Think of it."

"You might," I said, stealing another glance at The Belly That Ate the World. "You're pretty gigantic."

"And sure, I'll love him or her or them . . ."

"Barf."

". . . but I wouldn't love *you* less, dumb shit. You love Baby-Jon, I think, but it doesn't mean you love me less, right?"

I was weakening. "You leave the PoopMeister out of this."

"My heart is infinite. That means—"

"I know what it means, you whore."

"I'm gonna repeat, because I know all about your attention span and short-term memory: I won't love you less. Regardless."

"Well, it's about damn time! Thank you for finally putting my terrible hideous fears to rest. Was that so hard, reassuring me? Don't you get it?" I cried. "*I'm* the victim here! Everything's different but I'm the only one who knows it! I'd think you'd be a lot more understanding, given the situation."

The corner of her mouth twitched again. Her eyes, tilted at the ends like a cat's—she had beautiful eyes—narrowed, and then she gurgled laughter. She laughed so hard and so long, she had to lean on me to keep from falling down.

I didn't mind.

"Some things," she finally gasped, "never ever change. Including you, Bets, you selfish turd. I'm glad you didn't die again. Or stay dead."

"Well." I was mollified, but had no idea why. Maybe because she was leaning on me literally *and* figuratively? Or maybe because it was nice to have her to myself, even if it was only for five minutes. "I'm glad, too. So what *are* the odds of you having a litter?"

"Shut up," my best friend said, kindly enough.

TWENTY-NINE

"Okay, come on. I gotta hit the closet." I slowed my usual galloping pace while Jessica gasped and labored up the stairs. Being pregnant in a mansion this size must be a real bitch. All our staircases looked like something out of *Gone With the Wind.* "My clothes closet, not the water closet, which I have clarified because in this timeline you've become obsessed with going to the bathroom."

"Shut. The fuck. Up," she gasped.

"Hey, I can do a Rhett. Thinking about these stairs reminded me. I can scoop you up and sweep you up the stairs, except without a romantic lesbian vibe."

"Eat shit. And. Die."

"It'll be quicker. Probably. Even with my superior vampire strength, I'm not sure I could heft your bulk up these stairs."

"Touch me. And. Die."

Finally, she made it, and I followed her down the hall to my room. "At least we've gotten that out of the way."

"What out of the way?"

"You having the nerve to fall in love and get pregnant in an alternate timeline. I'm glad I've forgiven you; now I can concentrate on saving the world and, also, Marc."

"Jesus God," my friend muttered. I gently shoved her into a sitting position on my bed and darted into my closet. I couldn't save the future and also Marc and maybe beat up the Antichrist unless I had the right footgear. Sure, it sounded lame, but if I felt sexy and confident I could get more done. And these shoes made me feel sexy and confident. They were my version of a 1980s power tie, except not stupid. Case closed.

Except.

Um.

Sexy . . . and . . . confident . . . except . . . what?

"Wh-where . . . ?"

Jessica had rolled off my bed, stretched up on her toes, stepped closer and peeked over my shoulder. "What's wrong?"

"There's . . . there are shoes that should be in here that

are not in here. And there are shoes in here that should not, should not, should not, *should not* be in here!" I actually had to fight down the urge to throw up in my mouth.

There were over a dozen shoes missing, and my closet was a third full with . . . ugh . . . I could hardly . . . it was impossible and yet the grisly evidence was all over my closet. "What are all these velvet clogs doing in there?"

"Well. They're . . . you know." Jessica looked puzzled and alarmed. She covered her belly with both hands this time. Again, I was certain she had no knowledge of it. "They've been in for the last year. You—the you who was here a couple of days ago—you had just bought that navy blue pair, over there."

"But—" In this timeline I kept my good taste up my ass? Both Antonias were still dead but I now collected clogs? "But I hate clogs!"

"Since when?"

"Since always! And where are all the Christian Louboutins? I need my honeymoon Louboutins, my red Pavleta flats, I need them, where are they, I need them!"

"Your what?" Jessica, who had never feared me, ever, was backed all the way into the far corner.

"Pavletas, my Pavleta Louboutins, the Christian Louboutins, there should be twelve pairs of goddamned Christian

Louboutins in here and they're gone and I really need the ones I got on my honeymoon; *where are my Christian Louboutins!*"

"Who," Jessica asked, frowning so hard her forehead laddered into dark wrinkles, "is Christian Louboutin?"

My screams brought Marc and Sinclair on the run.

CHAPTER
THIRTY

The doorway actually splintered . . . Sinclair had been in a hurry. He didn't pause for a dramatic kick, he didn't sock his shoulder against it like they sometimes do in movies, he just crashed through it. You know those cartoons where the character runs through the door, and the door splinters into the shape of his silhouette? Like that.

He and Marc found me lying in the closet with Jessica rubbing my wrists like Doc Olson in an episode of *Little House on the Prairie.* "Ma Has a Heart Attack," maybe. Or "Laura Has PMS."

"I can't take it, I can't, I absolutely can't take anything else, it's too much," I gasped. "Tilt! Overload."

"You better take a breath," Jessica warned.

"Why? What possible good would that do except make me dizzier?"

"Point," she admitted. "Sorry. I forgot for a second."

"Sinclair loves me here." I was staring at the (water-stained) ceiling. "Sinclair loves me in this timeline and in the old one, and he loves me here and we're still in love here because he loves me here, so everything else can get worked out because he loves me, so it's okay, it's okay, don't be scared, it's all fine."

"Thaaaat whole thing?" Jessica worried. "That was all out loud, Bets."

"Who is it? Is it the Antichrist?" My husband was looking everywhere, all white around the eyes like a horse about to bolt, or stomp. "If she dared touch you again, I will—"

"What the hell!" Nick shouted, looking all 1970's cop, with his gun drawn and standing in the (battered) doorway. "Jess, get away from her! Are you okay? Why are you both in the closet?"

"Get away from her?" Freshly outraged, I sat up. "That's a nice way to talk to your landlady. Or the woman having sex with your landlord. Which is it in this timeline? Ooooh, I hate this timeline." I laid down again, moaning.

"It's, um, she's okay." Jessica coughed. "Relatively speaking."

"What happened?"

"What's wrong?"

"Bets, I'm not going to try to take your vitals this time,"

Marc said, pushing past Nick and kneeling beside me. I was instantly comforted by his cool-yet-warm bedside-y manner. "You can see me all right, yes, honeybunch? You don't feel sick? Or light-headed? Or deader than usual?"

"No, but don't call me honeybunch."

Feeling my neck, he laughed. I reached up and snatched his hand; we both pretended he didn't flinch back. Guess I'd moved quicker than I'd meant to. It always startled the hell out of people.

I had no choice, I had to confide in him. Call it a cliché, but only a gay man could understand my pain and, possibly, Beverly Feldman. "Marc, there's no Christian Louboutin here. He doesn't exist here!"

Marc winced and tried to loosen my grip. "Ow, ow, ow! Um, I think—yeah, you might have broken at least two of my—who's Christian Loobuhtohn?"

"Loo-boo-TAHN. Sorry." I loosened my grip but couldn't bear to let go. "He's just the . . . just the most brilliant shoe designer . . . he's a genius. Was a genius. Is he dead? Did he never get born? Poor Monsieur Louboutin!"

"You're carrying on," Nick observed, still watching the corners of the room in case a boogeyman leaped at us, "like he was a family member."

"I wish. I would have loved it if he were my older brother—he's in his forties now, so he'd be my much older brother. And he was born in France, right? And he'd sneak out of school—starting in seventh grade!—to watch the Paris showgirls, and he loved their high heels. Okay, that makes him sound like a little perv, but he's an artist, dammit. So he dropped out of school to be a shoe designer and he thought up the red sole."

"What's a red soul?" Dickie-Nickie asked.

"Sole. He does—did?—a signature red shoe bottom, which was a great idea, and when I left my timeline he had paperwork into the US Trademark Office so he could trademark the red soles. Killer, right?"

The tapered heel, slick colors, and splashy-yet-subtle red sole were fabbo enough, but last month I'd been able to buy his new ones . . . zipper heels! Black stiletto pump, red sole, zippers bisecting the heel, complete with tiny silver pull tab. God, why hast thou forsaken me?

"If this was anybody else," Marc was saying, "I'd recommend a transfusion and iron tablets. You don't fool me, blondie, I know you're light-headed."

Of course I was. "You guys! He almost singlehandedly brought stilettos back into fashion in the 1990s. He designed the shoes I wore on my honeymoon when I almost got killed. And he doesn't exist here." I started to cry. This alarmed everyone. Which, lamely, I found comforting.

"They were red flats and they were so beautiful because

they looked great but also I could run in them and they meant a lot because I got them on my honeymoon, which I didn't think I'd have but I did finally after stupid Sinclair finally agreed to really get married." I wept harder.

"You can't remember to swing by the store and get milk," Marc said, "but you know some shoe guy's entire biography?"

"Okay, saving you just dropped off my to-do list." I sniffled and sat up. "Dammit. Crying's not going to bring him back. It's not gonna fill my closet up with shoes that don't blow. Garrett's alive but there are no Christian Louboutins? It's like *Sophie's Choice*."

Marc patted my hand. "That's the spirit."

CHAPTER
THIRTY-ONE

"Do not think for a moment I am heedless to your pain," Sinclair said as we were all heading down the stairs. I braced myself because that was usually man-speak for "I'm about to say something that will annoy the shit out of you." "But where is the vampire?"

"The Marc Thing," I said, and Jessica nodded.

"Yeah, it's weird but it fits. And I can actually hear the capital letters."

"What can I say?" Marc said. He looked uncomfortable yet intrigued. "I die and become a badass."

Uh. Not exactly. You did because I either turned you or didn't save you. And then I rewarded your years of friendship with decades of torture, and then wouldn't put you out of your misery. I just let you roam around my Shitty Future Winter compound, scaring the hell out of people while I raise zombies and wear gray dresses. *Gray dresses!* Jesus wept.

(Wait, should I have written that in the future tense? Was it even the future tense? Present tense, I think. Maybe I should have written in past tense, since I was thinking about things that I *had* done, which I *will have* done. Dammit!)

None of that was out loud . . . I'm not quite as dumb as people sometimes thought. Probably. Maybe.

"He's still in the basement . . . I checked on him right when you guys pulled in."

"Whoa, wait." I stopped, and Marc plowed into me; I had to clutch at the banister so I wouldn't pitch headfirst down the stairs. "Don't get me wrong, you guys, I'm glad you came to get me, but you left a pregnant woman with no superpowers to guard the Marc Thing?"

"And Garrett."

I didn't say anything. I assumed Garrett was on guard duty in the basement while we were having this uncomfortable conversation in the middle of the stairs. But he was a coward, and flighty. At least, in my timeline he had been. What had he said earlier? His lover was dead, so there wasn't anything to be afraid of anymore. Sure. Except maybe there was. In my timeline, I hadn't been able to trust him. But I had no idea if that was true in this one.

He might *not* be in the basement. He might be curled up in a corner, shivering. He might be halfway to Hollywood . . . he'd been an actor in life . . . cast in *Gone With the Wind*! How cool, right? But died before he could show up for filming, which was a huuuuge blow to me, since that was one of my favorite books and movies of all time.

That was the thing about crazy chickenshits. They were unpredictable. Except when they weren't. Argh, I was getting a headache.

"So that was the plan? Garrett and Jessica?" I'm not judging Garrett. (I'm not! Truly. So don't judge *me*.) If I'd been through what he had, I'd be a shivering emotional wreck who fled from confrontation, too. It wasn't about judgment, it was about practicality.

Speaking of practicality, my conscience piped up, *you weren't here. You let your dumb ass get yanked into hell by the Antichrist, which, since she's the ANTICHRIST, you should have anticipated. They did the best they could—Sinclair had no way of knowing how much manpower he would need, and since his first priority was you, and not Jessica's safety, he erred on the side of caution. So enough with the Monday-morning quarterbacking, you useless cow.*

God! My inner voices were so *bitchy*. If someone outside my head talked to me like that, I'd string them up by their appendix.

"Our options were limited. Your mother was out of town," Tina said dryly. Hmmm, she must be more rattled than she let on. She usually didn't say shit . . . certainly when she was sarcastic there was almost always an undercurrent of respect and affection. Not this dry, clipped, irritated tone. "And when I looked in the Yellow Pages for ancient-vampire babysitters, the only listing was closed for the weekend."

"Would that be an ancient vampire who is also a babysitter?" Marc wondered, and Nick and Jessica both laughed. "Or is that, in fact, a babysitter for an ancient vampire?"

"Hilarious." Hmm. Pissier than ever. I resisted the urge to shout something lame like, *How dare you?* or *You're forgetting your place, Tina*, even though she'd be the first to agree with me. The last thing I ever, ever wanted to do was buy into this whole kiss-the-vamp-queen's-ass-every-five-minutes thing. That way led to dead friends and gray dresses.

"My mom . . . thank goodness I've *got* one in this timeline. Is she still watching BabyJon for us?"

Sinclair nodded.

"Maybe I should check on her."

"Do you think Dr. Taylor is in danger?"

Okay, I'm going to pause a minute and say I loved that my mom—a prof at the U of M—kept her married name. As long as the Ant lived (and after), that drove her nuts. Meanwhile, my mom was all, "You're welcome to my husband, but my name is mine. I've been a Taylor far longer than a Frend-sunverm" (my mom was German/Dutch).

"I don't know," I admitted. "But I'm wondering if Laura would go there . . . She knows where my mom lives. And she's keen on mastering her from-hell amazing teleportation trick. Plus, BabyJon is her half brother, too. You know she's gotten into her head that all vampires are soul-sucking, evil denizens of the undead. Sometimes that prejudice gets the best of her."

"Speaking of prejudice," Marc said, " 'shut up, you lesbian slut?' Was that homophobia rearing its ugly head?"

"I don't know," I said truthfully. We'd been tromping down the stairs this whole time, but now I was headed to the back entry for my car keys. Well. Sinclair's car keys. He had seven of the stupid things. "So we've gotta figure that out, too, I guess. But I'm not letting another minute go by without making sure my mom's okay."

"I doubt Dr. Taylor is the Antichrist's focus," Tina commented.

"I agree with you, but come on, guys. It's my mom."

"Call her."

So I stopped in the kitchen long enough to grab the phone—a rotary dial! What century was this again?—and dialed my mom's number. It rang four times and kicked over to voice mail.

"This is Dr. Taylor. I don't care why your paper is late, I'm failing you. If you are not one of my students, I'm away from the phone right now." Click. Terse, yet funny. Ah, my mom in a nutshell.

"It's the wee hours of the morning," Marc protested. "She's probably asleep."

"Not her." My mom was a notorious insomniac, not to mention one of those types who only needed four or five hours of sleep a night. Try growing up with *that*. "It's five a.m., honey, time to get up and mow the lawn. Of course you'll be able to see. The sun will be up any minute now." Hell, my teenage years had been a living hell!

"Well, okay. Try her cell," Marc suggested.

"She hates them." I was already sliding into my winter coat, a big down-filled thing that made me look like a midnight blue Michelin Man. Unseasonably warm autumn or not, I was always cold. "Refuses to have one."

"Text—no, wait, that won't work, will it? E-mail her."

"She never checks it on the weekends."

"With all respect," my husband said, and I mentally girded my loins, "your mother is a Luddite."

"Watch it, pal. That's your mother-in-law you're talking about."

"Tell me," he sighed. "I prefer not to let you out of my sight, dear one, but I . . ." He glanced around at our friends.

I knew what he was thinking . . . he was afraid to leave them, and he was afraid to let me go alone.

"I can be there and back in an hour," I promised. "I'll just check and come straight back."

"*Straight* back."

"Yep."

"Be careful," D/Nick said, and he was again cradling a protective arm across Jessica's shoulders.

"You know it," I said, and I went.

CHAPTER
THIRTY-TWO

So off I went, hopping on 94E and then 61S to Hastings. As I whizzed past the disturbing number of strip malls along the Woodbury/Cottage Grove stretch, I reminded myself that lying in general was bad, but lying to yourself was suicidal. So I wasn't deluding myself: I was glad to have an excuse to get out of there.

Not that I didn't want to be around my friends, or my husband. But too much had happened in just a few hours . . . and that wasn't counting my yuck-o time-travel adventures. Something mundane like checking on my mom was comforting, even though I was checking on her to make sure the Antichrist hadn't kidnapped her and my brother, or stabbed them with her Hellfire sword, or read Bible passages to them, or cajoled them into spending Thanksgiving Day working in a soup kitchen.

Ugh, T'giving. I almost forgot. I'd almost managed to forget. Gads, I hated that holiday. And for the record, I hated it long before it was trendy to despise the celebration of the genocidal slaughter (was that redundant?) of Native Americans whose dumbest move had been feeding Pilgrims so they didn't starve, instead of filling them with arrows.

It seemed to me that, call me paranoid, Thanksgiving was a holiday custom-made to piss me off. Traditional family gatherings? What traditional family? What *family*, for that matter? Even if my dad had really, really wanted to see me over T'giving, the Ant always talked him out of it. My mom refused to celebrate the genocide of innocent natives, etc., etc. Jessica's parents had, thank God, died in November, so she *really* didn't like November holidays . . . that wasn't completely true; she had no problem with Veteran's Day, come to think of it.

Laura's adopted family celebrated by not being home and not eating together as a family . . . soup kitchen central, which is lovely on paper but the reality is, you're on your feet all day serving cheap food to desperate people. I did it once and, yes, I'm a selfish cow, but never again. I ended the day slinking home and considering suicide by too much dark meat.

Boo-hoo, right? Yeah. I'm aware of how all that sounded. And I could make new traditions with my husband and brother/son, and Jessica and Dee-Nick's new baby, and Tina and Marc. But that would involve maturity, thoughtfulness, and making a concerted effort *not* to loathe T'giving, and the whole thing just sounded exhausting.

Despite my pissy fulminations, my spirits rose when I pulled onto Fourth, my mom's street, and headed toward her neat and clean two-story. Hope my mom had finally gotten around to baby-proofing . . . BabyJon would be walking before much longer. Probably. I should really crack a baby book one of these days. I had no idea what milestones to obsess about with other sisters/moms.

Just the fact that BabyJon was with my mother was cool, and odd. In the early days, Mom had had zero interest in babysitting her dead husband's love child. (He, Laura, and I all had the same dad.) But sometimes unavoidable vampire shit came up and she'd grudgingly comply so I could help the Antichrist kill a serial killer, or rescue Sinclair from a dungeon full of evil librarians and pissed-off werewolves.

But as the weeks turned to months the l'il shitbox had charmed her . . . he was a very good baby, and only cried when he was hungry or cold. Cute as all hell, too. Mom had actually volunteered to take him for the weekend the day before Laura and I disappeared . . . I hadn't had to ask her.

Which turned out great, seeing as how I went to hell the next day. But I digress.

Now I needed to see him, wanted to hold him and study his cute fat baby body, and marvel at the infant who technically wasn't my son, the baby I knew would grow into an admirable man in the future. The only son I would have, ever.

Was part of my problem with Jessica's pregnancy simple jealousy? I had to admit that it was . . . I was selfish, but not deluded.

And I'll admit it: I missed him! Granted, once he was around for a couple of hours and had shat his way through all the diapers in the bag and barfed pea puree all over my sweater and then wriggled to Sinclair's Cole Haans and slobbered Enfamil drool into them, I would no longer miss him. But right now, I did. So here I was.

I pulled up to my mother's small house in Hastings, a cute city right on the Mississippi River. My mom's house was in Cowtown, a holdover from when the area was a big field full of (you guessed right) cows.

Minor digression: what *is* it with people letting animals dictate major roadways or sites for major cities? In Boston they paved the cow paths, saying, "Hey, if it's good enough for slow-witted grain-grinding bovines, it's good enough to hold the city for the next four hundred years," and called it I-93.

In Mexico, they observed an eagle eating a snake while

perched on a cactus and said, "Guys! You guys! We should *totally* build Tenochtitlan here!" and bam! Up went another enormous city. Because of the cactus. And, I guess, the snake. After all, what are the odds of seeing a cactus and a snake in the desert, with a desert eagle?

Don't even get me started on the whole let's-build-the-nation's-capital-in-the-middle-of-a-steamy-swamp thing about DC. I just . . . I don't know. People think I'm not the sharpest knife in the drawer, and they're right, but I'd never build a ginormous city without, you know, *first doing some research.*

Okay. Digression over. I sprang from my car, almost jogging around it in my haste to see mom and son/bro, but skidded to a halt the minute my feet touched her front walk.

A man was there. On the sidewalk right before the big glass-cut front door. Kissing my mother. *Tongue* kissing my mother. On her own sidewalk! And why was a strange man leaving my mom's house before dawn? Was I witnessing . . . oh my God . . . was this a booty call? *Was my mother his booty call?*

Before I even knew I'd taken a step, I had my fingers sunk into his left shoulder. "I don't care who you are, you've never been closer to being murdered in a really grisly way." I yanked. He flew. Mom shrieked.

THIRTY-THREE

"Elizabeth Anne Taylor!"

I'm a grown woman. I'm thirty (forever). I haven't lived at home since I was seventeen. I balance my own checkbook and it comes out right (nearly every time).

I've survived the Miss Burnsville Pageant. I survived freshmen orientation at the U of M. I died. I came back. I'm married. I've been to hell. I've been to LA. I've been assaulted. I've been audited. I've messed with serial killers, zombies, scary vampires, lame vampires, vampire killers, killer vampires, werewolves, my stepmother, Satan, the Antichrist, killer librarians, cancer, knock-offs, and the absence of Christian Louboutin in this timeline.

I am the foretold queen of the undead.

Still, when my mom roared all three of my names, everything in me stopped dead and sort of shriveled up. Suddenly I was fourteen again, nailed red-handed lifting my mom's gold card because Jessica's driver was going to sneak us over to the Gaviidae Mall.

And here she came, stomping down the sidewalk, my sweet, "frail" mother, Professor Taylor. Her doctorate was in history, specifically the Civil War. When people asked, as they almost always did, "Are you a real doctor?" she'd reply, "No, I'm a hologram." My father, long before the divorce, had once told me, "Your sarcasm didn't come out of a vacuum." It was years before I figured out what he meant and by then, of course, he'd tired of sarcasm from any quarter.

I could see her jaw flexing from here; this was a Level Five Tooth Grind. The last time I hit a Level Five was when I ran over our neighbor's foot while I was backing out of the driveway. Then I ran over it again when I popped Mom's car into drive to rush forward to find out what he was screaming about. In my defense, he was a smelly bigot who referred to Jessica as "that little colored gal you run with" who always "borrowed" our Sunday paper. I'd had my driver's license for eighteen hours.

(And, while I'm thinking about it, colored? Seriously? Dude, it is not 1955, so pop some Tic Tacs and go lie down until you can remember that.)

(Oh, and the best part? Jessica laughed her *ass* off when I told her I couldn't hang with her for three weeks, due to the accidental squashing of the bigot's feet. She rushed over to his place and solicitously inquired after his health and asked to sign his cast and he was so freaked out that there was a gorgeous colored girl in his house he let her do it. "With love from your favorite jungle bunny." That was how she signed it.)

"You will pick up and brush off and apologize to Clive *this minute*."

Oh, right. Mom was mad about the schmuck I'd found giving her mouth to mouth. And possibly a close-chest massage, the perv bastard. After what I strongly suspected was a booty call. I wanted to very, very badly to bite someone.

"This minute," she repeated, like I'd died and come back and gone to hell and come back deaf. When I would have preferred coming back blind. Oh why oh why couldn't I be blind? "Nuh-uh. Who is he and why was he putting his germ-laden mouth on you?"

One heel tapping. Hands on hips. Yep, I was definitely closer to death than usual. Mom's eyes were lasers. "You're not funny, young lady."

"I'm a little funny," I mumbled, resisting the urge to scuff a toe in front of me as I stared at the sidewalk. "Sometimes."

I squashed the urge to obey. Somebody owed me an explanation.

Exasperated and super-pissed, my mom leaped forward to help . . . Clive, was it? Rhymed with jive, alive, and beehive. I decided that wasn't a good sign. Cliiiiiive. Gah.

For the first time I noticed she was dressed up—and this was a woman who, the minute she got tenure, was famous for lecturing in sweatpants. She was wearing a black mid-calf broomstick skirt with a crisp white blouse under a blue cardigan. She had her favorite locket on; in my timeline it held my teeny senior picture. I imagine Cliiiiiive's pic was in there now. Her face glowed with a fresh application of Jergens for dry skin. Also, she was wearing her Curious George slippers . . . a special occasion indeed!

So, fully dressed . . . my mom's version, anyway. In the wee, wee hours of the morning. So she'd been up all night with Cliiiiiiiive, or they'd both recently gotten up and gotten dressed. Curse you, logical brain, stop sniffing out clues that this was indeed a booty call! Go back to sleep, brain.

Don't let the white curly hair fool you—my mom's hair started going white in high school, and she still only had about three wrinkles. Instead of making her look old, her hair made her striking; I can remember being a kid and wishing I had white curly hair instead of stupid flowing blond waves. Mom got knocked up with me a month after graduation. She was fifty years old now—barely—and took care of herself.

I was not unaware that my mom was near Cougartown. The curly hair and the blue eyes masked her intellect and her formidable will. This was a woman who lost her husband to his secretary (cliché!), and spent the rest of their lives punishing them in a thousand small, aggravating ways.

"Wow," stupid Clive was saying. Mom had helped him up, which was great, because no matter how much she clenched at me, I wasn't gonna. Nope. He looked a little shaky, which was too bad. I wanted him a little comatose. "You're quick! You must work out. You must be Betsy."

I gave him a bright, white smile. "And *you* must be—"

"Elizabeth!"

"—Clive." What? That's what I was going to say all along. I swear on the soul of Clive, even if it means he had to burn in hell forever and ever if I had lied to myself just then.

"It's funny we haven't met before now." He extended his hand.

"Hilarious."

I stared down at his soft pink hand. He was the least dangerous-looking male I'd seen; in fact he looked like a giant baby. A giant baby who wanted to make out with my mom.

His rosy cheeks got pinker while I looked at his hand and thought the thoughts of an evil undead vampire queen.

Bad idea. One squeeze—not even a hard one for me—and you'll have toothpicks for bones. One twist, and you could be the one-armed man from The Fugitive. *Maybe two. You can't molest my mother with two dislocated shoulders, right?*

"I'm sure your manners will quickly return," my mom said. The finished sentiment: *They'd better.* I could actually hear her teeth grinding together: *krrrk-krrrk-krrrk.*

"Your reputation precedes you . . ." He turned to my mother and didn't smile with his mouth. But his watery blue eyes crinkled in a friendly way. He had a soft round face, and was plump the way men in their fifties had softened. Not fat, just . . . puffy. He was trying to be nice, but he was also nervous (yay!); when he swallowed, his prominent Adam's apple dipped up and down a little. He looked like he'd swallowed a cork. Why couldn't I have been the one to jam that cork down his throat?

The little hair he had was brown and wispy. He was wearing grass-stained black slacks, a grass-stained black dress shirt, and a grass-free white tie. Jeez, was he in the Mafia? "She's charming!"

And you're suicidal. I decided there was a possibility she'd grind herself into a stroke, so I shook his hand . . . barely.

You know those lame, clammy, limp-fingered handshakes that are just sad? That's what Clive got.

"Dr. Lively was on his way out. But you're on your way *in,* young lady."

"Yeah, Mom, I know, I'm the one who came *here*—wait. His name is Clive Lively?" Now I *really* wished I'd dislocated his shoulder. Or his face. "Oh, boy. The hits just keep on coming. Clive Lively. Nice to meet you, Lively, I'm going into my house to kill myself, hope you don't get run over six or seven times by a truck in our driveway."

So I did. At least the first part of that sentence, for sure.

CHAPTER THIRTY-FOUR

When my mom came back from what I prayed wasn't a passionate, sloppy, sizzling, wet good-bye embrace with my new mortal enemy, Clive Lively, I was pawing through her fridge.

"Well! That was . . . where do I start?"

Diet Pepsi? Ugh. Milk? She was down to less than a quarter gallon. Bottles of water? My mom had never been one to buy and tote her own clear fluids. Diet root beer? Maybe if someone stuck a gun in my ear.

"I know you've always had a flair for the dramatic, you terrible, terrible child, but that was bordering on felony assault." She stopped and frowned. "Mmmm. No, you didn't use a weapon. So just assault. Mmmm . . . no, it varies by state . . . What *is* Minnesota's stance on assault with intent but no weapon? I'll have to look it up."

Apple juice? Sure, if I wanted to drink something that looked like urine. Chai? No, I've never liked drinking something that tastes like Glade air freshener, no matter how much milk you dump in it.

"So, while I'm relieved you didn't produce a weapon, your behavior was still inappropriate and you will explain yourself."

Egg Beaters? What was I, stuck in a *Rocky* remake? I wasn't drinking raw eggs and running up and down a million steps for anybody. Ranch dressing? Oh, come on! This was getting sad.

"Nothing!" I slammed the fridge shut, then was startled when the thing rocked over a couple of inches. Stupid inhuman vamp strength brought on by the stress of watching my mom get pawed. If I could have gnashed my teeth without biting through my lip, I would have. "You've got a fridge full of nothing. The perfect end to a perfect day."

"Also, I'm fresh out of O negative," she replied, not in the least startled, tense, or afraid. If I'd picked up the fridge and threw it through the front door, I'd get a lecture on disturbing the neighbors. Vampires didn't scare my mom (she looooooved Sinclair, which, before I decided I loved him, too, was beyond irritating).

She stepped to the fridge, opened the freezer portion, then

pulled out a gallon bucket covered with several layers of Saran wrap. She shoved it at me like she was passing a basketball in the final five seconds, then pulled open the nearest drawer, extracted a soup spoon, and handed that to me. "There. Before you go foaming, barking mad and chase Clive down like a dog after a car wheel."

"Clive is a stupid name," I managed, because my mouth was already crammed with Mom's booze-free strawberry daiquiri slush. The Saran wrap was still drifting to the floor. I dug harder into the bucket. "And that's just for starters."

"I'll tell you what's for starters." She jabbed a finger in my direction. "Your explanation. Speak!"

She herded me over to the blond wood table I'd eaten at since I'd grown out of my high chair. Her kitchen was sunfilled (during daylight hours), bright, and sparkling clean. I'd never had her knack for, or interest in, house cleaning. All the appliances beamed at me like chrome gnomes. I could smell fresh vegetables, Windex, and my mom's Jergens. Familiar smells; I could feel myself start to relax and calm down.

I swallowed, took another bite, swallowed again. "Okay. You know how you offered to take BabyJon for a few days?"

"Yes, and you're lucky your nonsense didn't wake him."

"He is, too. He's had enough trauma in his life without running into Clive. God knows how long it is going to take *me* to get over it. Anyway, right after that, I had to go to hell, literally hell, with Laura. She needed help learning how to use her powers, and I needed help figuring out how to read the Book of the Dead without going nuts."

Mom was nodding. I knew that, as a historian, there was only one thing she loved more than talking to Tina about the bad old days, 1861–1865, beginning with Confederate dumbasses firing on Fort Sumter on April 12 and ending April 14, 1865, when Lincoln was shot. Not April 9, when Lee and the rest of the Confederate dumbasses surrendered. Mom considered Lincoln's double tap at Ford's Theater to be the last of the bad old days.

Before you freak out and decide I'm a Civil War Rainman, I got all this stuff practically with mother's milk. Literally with mother's milk, now that I think about it, because she was working on her doctorate when I was in preschool, so the ABCs I learned were a little different from most four-year-olds'. A is for Antietam. B is for Buchanan (James). C is for Confederate States of America. D is for Davis (Jefferson). Like that. I should have realized the funny looks I got in preschool were just the beginning.

Anyway, the only thing my mom liked more than grilling Tina ("What was General Lee *really* like?") was trying to figure out how to get the BOD (Book of the Dead) analyzed and read. It took me forever to talk her out of wanting to borrow the disgusting thing. I couldn't remember the last time I'd had to use my tried-and-true tactics of shrill hysteria and on-my-knees begging for such an extended period of time. Finally, more to shut me up than anything else, Mom gave in and abandoned the idea of borrowing it.

But she wondered about it a lot. When she found out I threw it into the Mississippi River, I thought she was going to hit me in the mouth. (Stupid thing came back, though, and dry as a bone. It always comes back. It's like a student loan officer. They just find you.)

"Risky . . . deals with the devil, don't you know. I don't recall a single instant when the devil was outsmarted."

"Sure you can. 'The Devil Went Down to Georgia.'" Greatest country song ever.

"All right. One instance, probably because the man in question was a musical prodigy. But I can understand why you risked it." Mom had grabbed a spoon of her own and sampled a bit of the daiquiri. "It tells you what will happen—or it could, if anyone could read it for a sustained amount of time. You might have been able to save Antonia."

Still might, I thought but didn't say. It was best to keep that to myself for now. Telling Mom about my hellish road trip after the fact was one thing. Telling her I was going again was something else.

"A thousand years old!" She looked as jazzed as I'd ever seen her. "My God, the things we could . . ."

"Quit it. Anyway, what happened was, we ended up in hell, like I said, and we also ended up in the past. Specifically, Tina's great-great-great-grandma's past, and then Sinclair's past, and then mine, and then . . ." I paused. Mom took my new (un)life pretty well. Amazingly well, all things considered. But I thought it'd be safer and nicer to leave out the future. I was either going to destroy the world (or help my sister destroy it), or not. Either way, I wanted to keep Mom out of it. "Anyway, when I got back, it turned out some things are different here now. I'm kind of stumbling around an alternate timeline."

Mom frowned, sucking on her spoon. "You mean . . . a parallel universe?"

"No, it's the same universe, I just remember it differently." Maybe. "Anyway, when I left, you weren't seeing anyone."

"Oh. Oh!" She actually rocked back in her chair as she grasped what I'd said. "So you've never heard me—oh, heavens, no wonder you committed assault or felony assault—I have to look it up—on my lawn. Oh, poor Clive!" She laughed, the heartless tart. "Poor Betsy!"

"Yeah, poor me." I tried to pull the bucket o' daiquiri away when she reached for more, and got a sharp rap on my knuckles with her spoon. "Ow! You know, I *am* the queen of the vampires. Some people are afraid of me."

"Then you should set an example for your toothy brethren by playing nicely. Well! Clive and I have been seeing each other for three months. You've heard all about him, but have never met him—the odd hours you keep, child. Yes? Yes. In fact, the four of us—your brother and Clive and you and I—were supposed to have dinner tomorrow night."

"Pass."

"What?"

She was gripping her spoon in an unfriendly way, so I clarified: "I have to find out what Laura's up to and also take Garrett to hell to find his dead girlfriend. And save Marc."

"Save *Marc*?" Mom's eyes went big. She'd met all my roommates. "Why?"

Dammit! This, *this* was how rattled I still was after meeting Clive. I'd planned on her not finding out about the future . . . which was a fine plan unless I forgot and *mentioned the future.* Jesus! I pitied, I really pitied the poor vampires who looked up to me as a role model, leader, and someone who can stick to a plan longer than sixty seconds.

"He becomes a seriously . . ." I paused, then used language I knew would get her attention, would prove how serious I was, language I never uttered lightly in this house. Believe it or not, I had been raised better than I turned out. "He's a fucked-up vampire in . . ." *The future. My future.* "What I mean is, the new timeline . . . there are things wrong with it." Oh boy, were there ever. "Look, it's a long story and I come off really bitchy in it. I'm trying to fix things . . . that's pretty much what it boils down to."

By the way, Betsy, you didn't run into Mom in the future, did you? Nice of you to finally realize.

I shoved that away. Mom not being in the middle of that winter wasteland a thousand years from now didn't mean shit, and now was not the time to freak out. About *that*, anyway. "Listen, just . . . if Marc ever comes here alone, don't let him in and keep your cross on." Mom had several. She had been collecting and wearing them as accessories long before Madonna made it trendy in the 1980s. "At all times have a cross on, okay? And don't let him in unless he's with Sinclair or me or . . . Sinclair or me. Unless we've talked to you."

I couldn't think of any reason the human Marc, our Marc, would come here alone. And I didn't have to think of a reason for the Marc Thing to show. He was crazier and scarier than a thousand Garretts. We couldn't even predict the weather, never mind the advance plans of psychos.

"Just protect yourself, and if you think you can't, or you run into trouble, or even if you can't sleep because you've got the creeps, *call me*. Or don't even take time to do that, just hop in your car and come over. Err on the side of caution, got it? There's tons of room at the mansion. What's another roommate?"

Mom snorted. She knew that while I liked/loved my roomies, I had preferred living alone.

"I've got no idea what happens next," I fretted. The bucket was nearly empty. Vampires were immune to brain freeze. No wonder people were scared of us. "Which pisses me off, because that's why I went to hell in the first place. So I could know what happens next!"

"Think that one over, Betsy. There's a reason Cassandra was both blessed and cursed by Apollo."

"Duh. Everyone knows that."

She ignored my bluff. "Cassandra was a princess so beautiful, the sun god Apollo gave her the ability to see the future."

"And I'm sure, given how the gods liked to run things, especially male gods, that there were zero strings to that 'gift.' She certainly wasn't expected to put out."

My mother smiled. "Cassandra was afraid, of both him and what he wanted to give her, and refused his advances. So he . . ."

"Turned her into a swan and had sex with her!"

"No, that's Leda and Zeus. What's the matter with you? Do you not have a good grasp of Greek mythology in the new timeline? Because the old you—"

"Oh, that's flattering. The *old* me. Great."

"Sorry. The other you from the other timeline knew all sorts of Greek myths."

"So do I!" I did, dammit. This, *this* was how rattled I still was. Curse you, Clive! May you be audited twice a year until the end of time. "Look, just run it down for me, okay? I'm on a schedule."

She wrinkled her nose at me. "Very well. Apollo let her keep his gift, but he fixed it so although she would know the future, no one would believe her until it was too late."

Ohhhhh. *That* Cassandra. Right. "What a lovely story. It wasn't depressing or anything. Thank you so much for sharing it with me."

"My point, wretched child, is that I think what Apollo did was a good thing. I don't think we should know too much about the future in general, never mind all the details of our own."

"Yeah, well, you're not the only one."

"Really?" Mom looked as surprised as I'd seen in a while. "That's curious, I always thought your husband would have—"

"I was thinking of Laura."

"Yes, I was going to ask you about that. How did she like hell?"

"A lot," I said glumly. "She's got wings in hell. Big pretty brown wings. And the first half dozen times she actually made a real effort to use her powers, instead of hiding from them, she did things I think only God should be able to do. What's she going to be like when she gets *good* at all that scary stuff?"

"Perhaps you should check the book."

"Can't. Laura took it and hid it."

"She did *what*?" Mom squawked.

I had to grin. That had been my exact reaction. "Yep. And she won't give it back. She said there are things I shouldn't know, and if there was trouble ahead, she was powerful enough to handle it, and if *she* wasn't, her mother was. Like I want Satan involved *any further* in my life! Or hers, frankly."

"Hmmm. That's very curious, isn't it?"

"Curious psychotic, curious maddening, curious I should make a citizen's arrest . . . what?"

"During your field trip to the netherworld, she understood you would have a new ability on your return, yes?"

"Sure."

"You finish your gallivanting through time. She helps you go home, then goes . . . where?"

"She can only teleport to different times and places from hell. She can get into hell, and then go somewhere else. But she can't teleport from, say, your living room to my kitchen. Hell's like . . . like the bus stop where she buys the ticket she needs to go where she needs."

"How poetic."

"You're the worst mother in the history of mothers."

"No, Medea has that distinction. And Diane Downs." Mom was a true crime fan; she thought Ann Rule pretty much invented the genre. "So am I to guess you don't know where she went once she dropped you off?"

"I made a few guesses, but I didn't know for sure."

"But some time later you called her, asked her to come over, yes?"

"Yeah." I was having trouble seeing where Mom was going. I knew all this, and now she knew all this, but what was the point of the rehash?

"Something happened between the trip back from hell and her visit to your home. Suddenly she doesn't think you should *have* the book, much less read it. That's what I call curious."

"So you're saying . . ." Uh. Nope. I still hadn't gotten there.

My mother took pity on her dunce cap–eligible daughter. "She found out something. Or was told something. And whatever it was, it had a radical effect on her attitude toward the book."

It took me a minute to catch on, but when I got it, it was like my brain suddenly gained weight.

"Holy shit!" I almost screamed. I was so shocked I didn't feel mom's spoon rap my knuckles again.

"Please." Wap! "A little decorum."

"The devil must have told her!" I held up my hand when Mom started to speak. "No, she didn't *find out* anything. The devil told her something big-time juicy, and then Laura . . . ohhhh, that bitch. Oh my God. Mom, you're brilliant."

"No, just logical."

"I gotta go. I gotta go ten minutes ago."

"You be careful."

"I'm trying. Sinclair's sticking pretty close. Except for right now, but that's my fault, not his." Sinclair. Nuts. I looked at my watch. "I said I'd be back in an hour, and throwing Clive across the lawn took up valuable time that I could have used eating more bucket booze. Gotta go, gotta go."

I stood. We wrestled for the nearly empty bucket for a moment, then I let her have it. There were just a few scrapings on the bottom left, anyway. "Remember what I said. Wear a cross, all the time. No outings with Marc. And Mom . . . keep the shotgun loaded and in your room when you're sleeping." My mom taught me how to hunt when I was a kid; she was one of the best shots in the state. She was to a twelve gauge what a gourmet chef was to shallots. "All the time, until I figure out what's going to happen. Or

someone figures it out for me." That tended to work pretty
well for me. No complaints.

"And you mind *me*, Elizabeth. I can't think of a single
myth or movie where someone found out their future and
didn't regret it. Laura may have the right idea."

"Traitor."

One thing about my mom . . . she was unflappable to
the extreme. When I came back from the dead she was so
overjoyed she didn't give a tin shit about the details. When
I explained I was a vampire, she was happy because it meant
I'd never die a mundane, preventable death (like, say, getting run over by a Pontiac Aztek).

Now I'd told her about visiting hell and the past, and
that she should watch out for a man she liked and trusted,
and explained a priceless artifact was in the hands of the
Antichrist, and that I'd be doing my best to confront the
devil as soon as possible. And all she had to say about all of
that was the Dr. Taylor equivalent of *watch your ass and keep
me posted, good-bye.*

"Want to peek on the baby before you go?"

I was way too tempted. "I better not. I'm already so
tempted to bundle him up and take him back with me." I
was tempted to tell her BabyJon grew up to be a fine man,
maybe even some kind of superhero since he was running
around a thousand years from now. And again, I held back.

It wasn't lost on me that Mom had mentioned more than once that it wasn't cool to know the future. She was making her stance on it clear to me, without coming out and saying it in so many words. "Give him a squeeze for me."

Mom smiled as she rose up and I bent down——she was a curly-haired shrimp——and she kissed me on the cheek. "That's part of parenting. When you do what's best for someone else instead of what you want."

"In that case, parenting blows."

She snorted. "Tell me." Then she waved. She waved until I'd pulled out, backed up, popped it back into drive, and was all the way down the street; she waved until I couldn't see her in the rearview anymore.

It was weird. I hadn't done anything, and I hadn't been able to give her any useful answers. In fact, I'd be having nightmares about Clive and the porch clinch for years to come. Still, I felt a lot better.

I guess even vampire queens needed their moms now and again.

I gritted my teeth and texted Sinclair I was on the way back.
Hate, hate, hate texting. In addition to being a ticket to a
body bag if you did it while driving, it was rude ("If you
don't put that down, I'm going to turn your phone into a
suppository."), and disruptive ("Darling, will you do me the
honor of becoming my—hold up, I'm getting a text from
my dog groomer . . . No! Look, *look* at the picture he sent
my phone! Mitzy is a poodle, not a dachshund . . . Do you
know how long it'll take her fur to grow back? Do you?
Huh?"). But it was beyond mean to let him worry. So I did
the dirty, dirty deed, then started the car and pulled out
of the driveway.

I never drive and text and, as far as I'd been able to tell, I'm the only person in the state who does this.

Twice in three months I had to stand on my brakes (Sinclair's brakes) and watch, stunned, as the driver cruised straight through a red light, their gaze glued to the teeny screen in their hand. Horns as Vengeance 101 tended to get their attention. I was tough to ignore during the best of circumstances (it's wrong that I'm proud of that), never mind when I was smashing my fists on the horn and leaning out the window to shriek, "Get your head out of your ass or *I will find you!*"

Whew. Just thinking about texting prevalence made me nuts all over again. If I were capable of it, I'd be having heart palpitations.

Quietly, from the backseat: "Hi?"

I screamed and heard the steering wheel actually groan as my grip tightened.

"Hi? Betsy?"

Then I made things worse by twisting around to see who was in my backseat. A serial killer, of course; the way my week was going there was no other explanation.

This is it. I'm about to be murdered and killed, which after meeting Clive I almost welcome. The regrets are eating me alive! I never texted Sinclair that I loved him; I only texted him I was on the way home. My texts are brutal; they're an emotional Arctic Ocean. Lord, please eventually let him find love again with a woman who isn't as hot as me.

The only question left was, did the killer behind me have an axe, or was one of his hands a hook? (You gotta love the classics.)

All this stuff happened in my head in a quarter of a second, and as a result while I was taking roll call for the backseat, I drove into a lamp post. The whole car shuddered and jerked to a stop with the impact. It rained glass for half a moment; things seemed very bright and fast, then dark and sluggish. The pool of light created by the street lamp vanished and it rained more glass. My seat belt tried its best to strangle me, and whoever was in my backseat was trying to induce my death by freak-out.

"Are you going to get Antonia now?" Garrett asked hopefully. "There's not much time left before sunrise."

"That's it? That's all you have to say to me?" I knew he was an uncomplicated and single-minded creature, but sheesh. "*You prick.* Why didn't you say something?" I unbuckled my seat belt, gave my car door a shove, then stood shakily in the street.

The hood was accordianed back almost to the windshield, and I could smell so much gas, oil, and hot metal it was almost unbearable. I didn't think the neighbors were in danger; I doubt any of them could smell it as strongly as I could. Didn't seem to be bothering Garrett, though, which I found annoying.

I coughed and swayed and said it again. "You prick. Lurking in my backseat? Are you out of your—scratch that . . . gah, Sinclair will not be pleased, and neither will our insurance company, Garrett, c'mon, jeez, I can't—you shouldn't— what the *hell*?" Hmm. I was sounding a little shrill. And feeling a little bitey.

"I told you I was in the back." He was calm and unruffled, if shy. Meanwhile, I felt like I might fly into a zillion pieces, all of them in a bad mood. "I told you the second you got in. You couldn't hear me. So I said it louder. But you couldn't hear me again."

I yanked on the car handle. I was going to haul him out by the scruff his neck and beat him to death with the streetlight. Or the passenger door.

"It's true," Laura said. "He was trying to tell you. I said hi, too, but you had that look . . . the my-brain-is-on-pause look. Did you know you sort of go away when people are trying to tell you things?"

"And then you snap back, and sometimes you've been able to follow the conversation and sometimes we have to help you," Garrett added.

I could only assume I had a skull fracture. What—

where—what was Laura doing here? "Good God!" Garrett climbed out; Laura slid out behind him. I bent and peeked. "How many people are back there?"

"Just us." Garrett was beginning to recover from my exclamation. Sinclair had once told me hearing God or Jesus or what have you felt like a whiplash. Across his balls. "We were waiting for you."

"Swell." I ran my fingers through my hair and closed my eyes, fighting the urge to yank. Or slap. "Where to begin? I'm so pissed at both of you right now I'm gonna stroke out. Must punish . . . and yell . . . too many emotions . . . arrgh, the pain!"

"Are you all right?"

"Noooooooooooooooooooo."

Laura coughed, a delicate *em-erm*, and said, "We were in the same car accident you were, and we seem to be doing all right."

That was a matter of opinion.

"Yes, but you caused the fucking thing! You knew you were in the backseat, but I didn't know you were in the backseat so I was startled to hear him in the backseat and then see him and then see you, you knew that would all happen but I didn't." I stared at the mess on the sidewalk. "Also, nitwits, my mom's a taxpayer in this town. She and everyone else are gonna get stuck paying to fix the light."

"Since when do you even know what taxes are?"

"Hey, great news, Laura, you just won! Here I've been wondering which of you to kill first. I'm now officially madder at you than him and will punish accordingly. To begin with: you suck. And your mom? The Lady of Lies? She lied! Again." You'd think I could predict this behavior by now.

People were opening their front doors to get a good look, and no wonder; the sound of the crash had ripped through the peaceful, small-town evening. I was willing to bet someone had called the cops. Hmmm, where *did* Sinclair keep his car registration? Because I had the feeling I was going to have to flash some paperwork. At least no one was hurt. Especially me.

"Yes, well." Laura couldn't look at me. Garrett had no trouble, but he wasn't nervous like she was. Just hopeful, like a basset hound watching someone open a box of jerky. "I, uh, I thought I might owe you an apology, you know, after what happened, but when I went to the mansion, Garrett met me in the driveway and we left for your mom's . . . to save time I took us to Hell first, then here. I never even made it inside. And I didn't want to see—I mean, you were the one I wanted to talk to, not the others. But we didn't want to bother your mom, so we just waited for you."

(Note to self: start locking the damn car.) I should have been happy. An apology? Great! We would now live happily ever after as mandated by every happy ending in the world. No point looking back; we'd just surge forward, etc., etc., hallelujah, amen.

But the needle on my Creep-O-Meter was bouncing. Not just because Garrett liked skulking in the front yard, and not because he'd had the courage to ask Laura to ride along (the Garrett in my timeline would have barely spoken to her, never mind asked for anything). No, the worst part was how Laura was willing to go straight to my mom's with a feral vampire, one she knew was damaged, one she knew was unpredictable and dangerous, one who, after being brutalized and killed didn't speak a word for something like fifty years. And then . . . then! Lurk patiently in the backseat. With an apology, no less. Then be surprised when I freak out.

"Laura . . ."

"I thought I was helping you. I really did. When I wouldn't give it back. You believe me, right, Betsy?" Her eyes were wide and the left one brimmed with a single perfect tear; she could have pled without making a sound. "Right?"

I chewed my lower lip and thought it over. Which in itself was a change; even a year ago I would have fallen all over myself to accept her apology, would have been glad of anything to keep, or return to, the peace.

Again: yes, I was very glad she'd come back repentant.

But this was one of her scarier qualities. She could go from sugar to boiling lava in eight seconds. And just as abruptly, her rage would leave her and she wouldn't hesitate to make amends. It was bewildering, and unpredictable.

And I had no choice. I had to forgive her, had to hug her and pretend some of the fight was my fault. Because I could not afford to go to war with the Antichrist.

Not yet. And it was awful that I was even contemplating when that step might be inevitable. If I had changed a bit in the last three years, so had my little sister. When we met, she'd never skipped church . . . now we were fortunate if she went twice a month. She'd never been in a fight, hardly ever raised her voice. But she'd killed vampires and at least one human serial killer.

To say nothing of the time she tried to kill *me*.

My point: I couldn't afford a grudge, which sucked because I was pretty good at holding them. So though it was tempting to cling to my righteous wrath, I nodded and gave her a quick A-frame hug (shoulders together, asses far apart) and told her it was all right, it was no big thing, the important thing was that she'd come to her senses.

Guess which two of those were the lies?

She hugged back so hard I could practically hear myself squish. Really hard, and instead of resting her hands on my back she had bunches of my shirt in both fists. She wasn't hugging so much as . . . clinging. Like she was drowning or something. Like I could save her.

"Okay, I'm glad you quit being such a mega—uh, I'm glad we got that straightened out. Listen, we've got to get back to the mansion and deal with the Marc Thing, but the car is—"

"Everybody okay?" someone called from across the street. I turned and gave them my Miss Burnsville wave.

"Just fine!" I lied cheerfully. "Thanks anyway." No vampires or Antichrists over *here*, no, sir. Just your standard car vs. streetlight.

"I thought we could use hell, since your car is wrecked."

"Eh? Oh." Our speedy yet invisible getaway from this suburban neighborhood; that was the topic to tackle. "Mmmm, gosh, tempting but . . . how about a cab instead? Or Sinclair can come pick us up and mourn his Jetta. I think using hell as our vehicle just makes things unnecessarily complicated." For some reason I was reminded of one of the best cartoons in the history of animation, *Up* (Kevin the bird was my fave, and Kevin's babies!).

At one point, the kid, Russell, says he'll take the bus from Paradise Falls back to his house: "Whoa, that's gonna be like a billion transfers to get back to my house." A hell-bound bus ride . . . how many transfers would it take to get back from hell?

"We're getting Antonia now."

I noticed that wasn't a question. Garrett wasn't contributing much to this meeting, except to startle me half to death and nag me to take him to hell. Beyond that, he clearly didn't give a shit.

"You said," he reminded me, like we were on the playground.

"Well, yeah, the me from the original timeline promised, but right now? Right this second right now?"

I didn't think Garrett was going to answer, but he did, and was I concussed or did he sound pissed? "If it was the king, would we stand and discuss?"

"But it's not the king." As soon as it was out, I could have jammed both hands over my mouth. Wow. Elitist much? The sneaky undead craft-mad knitter had a point. But then, so did I. Sinclair was the king; weren't things different for him by definition? For me?

I had no idea if I was right, and less interest in finding out. When I heard "not the king" come out of my mouth, the part of me that had no interest in becoming Ancient Betsy decided the discussion was going to go Garrett's way.

"I don't know if we can get her or not," Laura-I'm-not-a-killjoy-I-swear said. "There's so much about Mother's home I don't know. But I can at least get us there. Can help you talk to her and find Antonia."

"That's nice of you." This, in as neutral a voice as I could manage. Had she ever called Satan *Mom* or *Mother* before? Usually it was *her* or *my mother* or *that evil creature.* What was next? Mother's Day brunches? "I'm glad for the help and I'm sure Garrett is, too."

"You promised," he nagged yet again. He'd make Antonia a wonderful housewife. He could knit sweaters and hector Antonia about mowing the lawn. A regular 1950s family, with fangs. On both sides, come to think of it.

"Well, I really feel as though I have to . . . and I want to, also," she assured Garrett.

Hmmm. (I was hmmmming a lot these days.) In other words, *I'm sorry and please take advantage of my regret to help your lackey. This way you don't have to talk me into anything, won't that be nice?*

Her expression told a similar story: *I'm sorry, please let me do this. I'm sorry, sorry, so sorry.*

And she was. I believed that. She was sorry, sorry, so sorry. Until next time.

I hated fence-sitting, especially when I was the one doing it. Laura's offer was a time-saver at the very least. And since when did I turn my back on a shortcut?

CHAPTER
THIRTY-SIX

Hell is a waiting room.

I know: rerun, right? You've heard this before, because I've said it before. (Also: thanks for paying attention!) But I never ceased to find it weird and unsettling. Of all the things I'd expected—waterfalls of lava, flames, the shrieks of the damned, no parking, no returns, no way out, no hope, no refunds—a waiting room seemed anticlimactic at the least.

Even worse, my odious dead stepmother, the other Antonia, was at her customary place in hell: the assistant's desk, the place where, if this had been a CEO's office (which it sort of was), her right-hand gal would have sat.

But the Ant did more than greet the damned (or the just-visiting). She helped Satan with all sorts of things to lighten the load of running hell every day for many thousands of years. They weren't friends, but the Ant respected the bejeezus out of Satan, while Satan was grateful to the Ant for bearing her (Satan's) daughter.

Oh, and almost being friends with Satan? Keeping the devil's appointment book? Speaking of the Lady of Lies in glowing and respectful terms? I was the least surprised person in the history of human events to discover all that was true about my loathsome, revolting, detestable stepmother.

"Not a chance," she said by way of greeting. I was annoyed to see she appeared on top of things—she'd sucked at day jobs while she was alive, but was a terrific assistant in death—and pleased to see that she dressed even more badly in hell. Though maybe that went hand-in-hand with *being* in hell. "Run along, children. And you, whatever you are." Her nostrils flared as she eyed Garrett . . . skinny, tense Garrett.

"I want Antonia."

"You can't have me," my slutty stepmother replied primly.

To his credit, Garrett didn't groan and vomit. "The other one."

"I'm not sure this is the way to go about it," Laura murmured, laying her fingers on Garrett's forearm. "Just blurting it out like that."

"I want Antonia."

"I guess ignoring everyone's advice is another way to go," I commented, then turned to the Ant. "I'll take a cinnamon hot chocolate, extra whip, with whole milk."

"You've never been nearly as funny as you imagined."

"But you always managed to raise the bar when it came to being greedy and selfish. Go fetch yon boss, pineapple hair, before I show you I'm my mother's daughter."

She snorted. Which I expected . . . threatening her with my mother only worked in life. Not only was the Ant right not to fear my mom anymore, she probably didn't have to fear me, either. What I found most interesting, though, is that the Ant showed no shock at seeing us step through Laura's doorway into the waiting room.

Laura had to actually cut doorways through space with her Hellfire sword . . . I knew what it looked like going through, but I'd never seen it when someone came through to somewhere I already was. I hoped it was cool and dazzling. That would be a nice change.

The Ant, I couldn't help notice, hadn't moved to obey my command.

"Where's your boss?" I whined. "I gotta go shrill all over her ass."

"None of you have appointments or are expected, and my boss, as you uncouthly put it—"

"Uncouthly? Don't make up words. Uncouthly. Please."

"—is busy, which even Betsy should be able to understand. She's quite busy. Do you understand quite busy, Betsy?"

"Yeah, it's a state of being you've never endured." Ha! Take that, pineapple hair.

"Oh really? Busy is putting it mildly. There are over sixteen billion souls on this plane."

"Sixteen billion?" If I'd had to guess, I would have tried . . . I dunno . . . ten million? "Get out of town! Sixteen billion?"

"Sixteen billion seven hundred ninety-four million eight hundred twenty-four thousand and three."

"It's so weird and gross that you know that."

"And they all have needs, of course. Which is why we're set up here. To meet their needs."

"So they *need* to burn forever or whatever their personal hell is?"

"Exactly. We serve *them*. It's not the other way around. I'm told it's never been the other way around. All of which is to explain how busy the boss is. Of course," she added, her tone softening as she looked at Laura, "I'm sure she'll make an example for you, hon."

"Don't you mean she'll make an exception?"

The Ant flapped her press-on nails at me, subtly painted Screeching Whore Red. "That's what I said."

"Because that's kind of a big Freudian slip," I tried again. Why was I the only one who found that unsettling? Simple: Laura had nothing to fear in hell . . . who'd be psycho enough to try to harm her? And Garrett didn't care about anything, and could focus on nothing, until he had his werewolf gal-pal back in his big, strong, neurotic, undead embrace.

The Ant patted her tall yellow hair. "Don't use words you don't understand."

"Okay. I understand *pummeled*. I understand *maimed*. I understand *acid* and *burns* and *deface* and *mutilation* and *disfigure* and *scar* and *damage* and—"

"Please find out if Mother will see us," Laura asked with the flawless manners taught by her preacher dad. It was just as well . . . as fun as verbally kicking the Ant's ass had been (Yahtzee!), it wasn't getting us anywhere.

And there it was again. Mother. Not *my mother*. And was it me, or was Laura getting less annoyed when she spoke of the devil or found herself in the devil's presence or found herself manipulated into a course of action by the devil?

Because she used to hate it. Her. Whatever. But now, even if she wasn't seeking Satan's company, these days Laura didn't seem to *mind* the company, if you get where I'm going.

"At once," the Ant said, and disappeared like a soap bubble: shiny and silent. Garrett was staring straight ahead, almost vibrating, but waiting for a command like a leashed rottweiler. Laura was trying not to look pleased, and I was trying not to freak out more than I already had.

I took my phone out of my purse—I'd pulled the beat-up handbag (I was a shoe girl, but gave not a shit for bags) from my (his) wrecked car, slung it over one shoulder, and brought it to hell, though I'm not sure why. Maybe I thought I'd want to buy a hot dog while I was here, pay for a few rides?

I looked at my phone and told myself, again, that it was good I didn't let Sinclair know what I was up to. He'd freak, he'd order, he'd worry, he'd have a nervous breakdown, he'd yell at me from inside my head, then he'd yell at me in person. And the tiresome lecture when he found me again . . . I could feel myself yawn just thinking about the droning.

Also, he might have insisted on coming with . . . and Laura might have let him.

So I'd texted that I'd been delayed (truth) but would get back as soon as I could (truth) and there was nothing to worry about (untruth).

Because knowing he'd want to come . . . well. That made it easy. Sure, I was acting like a scary movie heroine, someone from, say, *Saw XXXVII*. I went to hell with the Antichrist and a feral vampire on the spur of the moment and didn't tell anyone where I was going. I deserved to have my head cut off or my face eaten or whatever a script writer (if my life were a horror movie, and I were a busty starlet) could think up. And it was all fine as long as it meant Sinclair was (relatively) safe.

Sinclair? In hell? No way. Only one Sink Lair family member was going to hell three times in the same week, and it *wasn't* the guy whose entire family had been murdered before he was voting age.

Oh. Oh. Oh. Did . . . did I just refer to myself as a Sink Lair? Have things gotten as dreadful as that? Back in hell in the same week looking for Antonia while dealing with the other Antonia (a hellish curse all its own), a summerless future lurking a thousand years down the road, no Louboutin shoes since there was no Louboutin, and now this? *Curse you, Satan, for poisoning everything you touch!*

"I gotta sit down," I managed, seconds before I did so. And for the first time I was glad hell was a waiting room. No shortage of chairs, so that was good. But they sure were uncomfortable and that, I figured, went with the territory.

THIRTY-SEVEN

"Unexpected guests," Satan called breezily as she swept in, the Ant right behind her. "Lucky, lucky me."

As usual, Satan looked beautiful and fearless. It pleased her to take the form of an older woman—a really gorgeous older woman—and as usual, her designer suit and shoes were dazzling. I tried to avert my eyes but, like Lot's wife (Laura told me who that was and what happened to her), I always, always had to check her footgear.

This time she was dressed in a smartly cut tan suit; it looked like wool. In hell! Well, I suppose if the heat didn't bother Satan . . . which, given her job description, made sense.

The skirt was a black high-waisted pencil skirt with the

hem stopping just above the knees . . . a risky move for an older woman (or fallen angels who chose to look like older women) but Satan had the legs to carry it off. The sleek jacket had long sleeves and crisply notched lapels. Her blouse was cardinal red and, from what I could see, silk, with a soft, almost scooped neckline and mother-of-pearl buttons. No makeup, no jewelry. And she didn't need either, dammit.

"To what do I owe this unexpected intrusion?"

I opened my mouth to answer, then looked at her feet again.

The devil was wearing my shoes. My red Christian Louboutin honeymoon flats.

My shoes.

The devil had my shoes.

The devil. Was wearing. My honeymoon shoes. In hell.

"Something catch your eye, vampire queen?"

I had no memory of deciding to move, of wondering what I should do. Somehow I'd made it all the way across the room while "catch" was coming out of her mouth. Somehow my hands were around her throat and squeezing. There was a dim sound behind me—like muffled waves hitting a beach made of cotton, not sand. Faint and not important.

I felt and heard the crunch as Satan's vertebrae shattered. Her eyes were brown and bulging. She had her hands locked around my wrists. Somebody had ahold of the back of my shirt and was trying to pull me back. Too late.

Then a distinct sound, one I couldn't remember ever hearing before but recognized all the same: death rattle.

Best sound ever.

CHAPTER THIRTY-EIGHT

The Ant and Laura had succeeded in pulling me off. This helped mostly because I stopped resisting them. They yanked back so hard I ended up sitting on the floor. Garrett still hadn't moved. When I glanced at him, wondering if I'd hear dismay or anger or fear or *something*, he said, "We're going to go get Antonia now, right? Betsy? Right?"

"Jeez, you've got a one-track mind." I wasn't as annoyed as I sounded. For one thing, I was still high from throttling the Lady of Lies. For another, if I were in his place I'd have the same focus. Well. That wasn't true; I could never, ever have that kind of focus. But I'd be anxious about Sinclair.

Sinclair! Thank you, thank you, thank you, God, thank

you he wasn't here. Thank you he wouldn't be here when Satan came to.

Because I wasn't kidding myself. There was no way someone who was once in the Miss Burnsville Pageant could have killed the devil.

I hope I startled the shit out of her, though. I hope the next time she thought about fucking with me, her neck throbbed like a rotten tooth.

"Look what you did!" The Ant was staring at the crumpled form of her boss, tossed in the corner like a new toy six months after Christmas. "You—I can't believe what you did!" The Ant looked scared and exhilarated. But mostly scared. She'd always had an easy face to read, and I could see her wondering about which way to jump.

The devil was the big boss in town; it was safe to align with her. But her bitchy entitled stepdaughter had just kicked Satan's ass all over Satan's waiting room. So maybe the balance of power wasn't as stable as she imagined. "What—what are you going to do next?"

"What, like I know?" Actually, I did know. I walked up to the (temporarily) prone body, bent, and slipped off first one shoe, then the other. I held them with the two fingers on my left hand. I could have put them on, but that would have meant abandoning my loafers (Ella Signature, Coach, black). With luck I wouldn't have to choose between them.

With luck. I could have rolled my eyes at myself. I just bitch-slapped the devil on her home ground and I was worrying I'd have to leave a pair of shoes behind? If I was *lucky*.

Well, I wasn't going to bitch (much). I wasn't going to whine and blame Satan and snivel to myself that life just wasn't fair for poor old me, boo-hoo, how come *my* life is so weird and dangerous and full of felony assault?

I wasn't going to indulge because a) I wasn't sorry, and b) I'd do it over again, which I guess is the definition of not sorry, and c) I was okay, probably, with sucking up the consequences of those acts.

"Oh. Oh, oh, oh. Betsy, what did you do?" Laura sounded shocked and scared. At least she wasn't avenging her mom by getting strangle-y all over my ass. And her wings had popped.

Okay, that probably sounded odd. Let me back up. Laura was the daughter of an angel. See, the devil's lineage didn't change when she moved to hell. (That was *her* story. Got kicked out and had to go to hell, that was my story.)

Anyway, Laura had inherited her wings. I didn't know if all those old painters were right (that angels were fair and gorgeous with snowy white wings and halos and long flowing robes), but this part *was* right. Angels had wings, half-angels had wings, Laura had wings.

They were lush and brown, like a sparrow getting ready

for winter. And it was obvious Laura hadn't noticed they were out. So I wasn't gonna tell her.

"What are we going to do?" Funny . . . Laura had asked the question, but she and her biological mother had identical expressions of dismay on their faces. Looking at Laura was like looking at the Ant and seeing what she'd looked like when she was young. The way she used hair dye and loud clothes and vivid makeup to look like when she was young. "Should we call for help?"

"Who would we call?" the Ant pointed out. Good questions. Glad it wasn't my problem.

What I thought was really interesting was that either the Ant saw Laura's wings and decided not to comment, or she hadn't noticed they were out.

Okay, I'd better explain *out*. The way I understood things, Laura always had wings . . . in hell, in the past, in the present, in the future. The way I always had my appendix. But people in an ordinary shithole realm like earth couldn't see them.

Hell wasn't necessarily a hot place beneath the earth's crust (though it was nice and toasty warm here in the waiting room). It was another dimension, with different rules and different people and different customs and different physics. As in, "Ye canna change the laws of physics, mohn!" Except since this wasn't earth, anything was possible.

Laura had been staring at me this entire time, and I could

tell she was torn. Yell at me? Help her mom? Yell while helping? Kick me in the shins? Flap and fly away? Call hell's version of 911? What?

None of us knew what to do, and that was a plain fact. Of the three of us, though, I was definitely in the best mood. I even hummed a little, waiting for them to decide what they were going to do.

"You . . . perfidious . . . violent . . . crude . . . hideous . . . wretched . . . *bitch.*"

THIRTY-NINE

The voice was raspy and weak and hissed more than spoke.
The voice sounded like nothing human, which made sense, because the person who owned that voice *wasn't* human. And check out the list of insults! The devil must have kicked ass in vocab.

Everything inside me went cold, while my face got warm. I figured out what that meant after a second . . . I was scared, yet pissed. I patted my warm cheeks (which, due to my sluggish blood flow, were almost never warm). Yep, definitely getting hot under the collar. Hmm, wonder what could have brought that on? I could feel the hairs on the back of my neck not just trying to stand up, but trying to get the hell out of Dodge.

I don't blame you, l'il hairs. We should all leave. So how dumb does that make me, that I'm just standing here waiting to be smited? Or whatever?

Satan was getting up. Carefully and slowly, she was rising to her feet. Her movements were stiff and forced. Her face was still a mottled blue; the whites of her eyes were severely bloodshot. No, they were filling with blood. No, they were red. The whites of her eyes were red. No. The whites and her pupils were red. It was like being glared at by a stoplight. A stoplight who had a run in her panty hose.

And her wings were out. They were red, too, cardinal red. They fluttered and seemed to help her with her balance as she climbed up from the floor into a standing position. They were huge . . . the top of the wings started just above her neck, and the tail feathers stopped just above the floor.

What I found really strange was that the wings and her new and improved eye color didn't make her seem alien or odd, though I'd never in my life seen someone (something?) who looked like that. In a weird way, seeing her wings pop made the whole package easier to swallow. It showed that the suits and the shoes and the carefully prepped hairstyles were the camouflage. The woman in this room with me now, that was the *real* Lucifer.

Weird, to look at something so alien and unfamiliar and think, *This is right. This is the way she's supposed to look.*

It made me think of Laura's eyes and hair . . . when she got mega-pissed her hair would deepen from blond to red, and her eyes would go from blue to poison green. It was like the coloring was her litmus test for rage. Maybe that's why I wasn't terrified when we fell through the library into hell and, for me, anyway, woke up on a coroner's table. Her hair and eyes had never changed. So at the time I knew she was pissed, but not, like, lethally so.

Lucifer finally got all the way to her feet—it seemed, at least to me, to take a long time. It also seemed to hurt. Awwww. The devil had a boo-boo. She clutched her head in both hands, then closed her evil scary red eyes and gritted her teeth. We could all hear them grinding together and then a new sound, a sort of dim crackle. It took me a second to realize: she was healing her shattered vertebra. They were knitting back together right in front of us.

My finger marks stood out like vivid red brands on her Anne Boleyn neck ("I have a little neck," remember? A great line for someone who knew she was going to be legally murdered by the thug who was Henry VIII). While we watched, the marks on her neck slowly faded . . . it was like watching a film run backward. Harsh marks, then lighter, then fading, then . . . look at what the miracle of plastic surgery can do for women of *all* ages!

"Wow, who could have predicted any of that?" I wondered

out loud. "Weird. Do you think it was something you said? Or something you did?"

Satan glanced down at herself, saw her skirt was rumpled and her panty hose had runs. Then her skirt was fine and her panty hose were flawless.

She looked at her bare feet for a few seconds, which seemed like years, and then simple black flats appeared, probably Dior.

I wasn't certain why she was taking so long to smite me, but I had an idea. An idea that might have occurred to her right around the time I was making her neck go squish.

I shouldn't have been able to hurt her, that was the thing. She was a zillion-year-old angel, she was *the devil* for crying out loud, and this was her world, her realm, her turf. No one ever tried to stomp her before? Ha. No one ever got the drop on her since God nailed her with His official smackdown? Double ha. No one ever tried to stomp her on her own turf before? And again, I say ha. Even if I took my considerable shortsightedness and vanity into question, I couldn't make myself believe that.

Not because I was a mega-powerful vamp queen. Because I wasn't especially original, and no one could tell me that in skatey-eight billion years, not one person had ever tried to pop Satan here in hell.

So I figured that had to mean one of two things. Lucifer let me kick the shit out of her. Or she didn't. And right now

I had no idea which one it could be. I almost wished Sinclair were here. He was pretty smart about the sneaky stuff. So was Tina. She practically had a master's in trickery. Either of them would have been able to figure this out by now.

I glanced at Garrett. I hoped the devil didn't hold grudges now that we were about to ask a favor. Then I almost laughed at myself *again*. I had never been the sharpest knife in the drawer, but I normally wasn't this naïve, either.

I cleared my throat. Peeked at Garrett once again. There was no chance, *no* chance, but I had to ask for Antonia anyway. I wasn't going to come all the way to hell and not even say her name. "So, you're probably all wondering the reason we're all gathered here today—"

Satan held up a finger. "You should not talk right now."

"I'm sure you're right, but that never has, and never will, be—"

"What do I have to do to get you to leave?"

Uh. What? *Get* me to leave? Like she couldn't throw my ass out whenever she wanted? Like she had to be careful because she might need me? Or I might fuck her up? Please. I hadn't even been able to make her dead for more than a minute. Maybe if I reeeally pissed her off she might have a stroke . . . for about fifteen seconds. There wasn't anything I could do to her that she . . .

She . . .

Okay. Wait. Vain as I was, I'd never believe I could hurt the devil, really hurt her. Not right *now*, at least.

But how about, oh, I dunno, let's grab a number at random. How about a thousand years from now? Hmm? How about *then*? Was I a danger to Satan after the world ended and I was king of the mountain?

Aw, shit. You know how when you think of something and have no evidence any of it's true, and no way to prove it will *be* true, but you know it is all the same? The way you know your name, and how your husband's hands feel on your skin? That's how it was. Even as I was speculating, I could almost feel the *click* as my brain engaged and coughed up explanations that felt right.

So: Lucifer was afraid of Ancient Me, or needed Ancient Me, or both, so she couldn't smite me anytime this year, or the next, or the next. So: she wanted us out of her living room (in a matter of speaking). So: what do you ask the devil for when you know there's not much she won't give you?

Naturally, my first thought was of Antonia (the least annoying one). That was why we'd come, and it was good that we came . . . I was beginning to see the wisdom in the old fortune-cookie saying ("Keep your friends close, but your enemies should be watched a lot," or however it went). Antonia should never have died in the first place. If I'd been quicker, or smarter, or bulletproof, she wouldn't have. And, at the time, if someone had said to me while we were all staring at her brains on the wall, "If you could undo this, would you?" then yes, I absolutely would. So here was our chance, and I wasn't going to waste it.

I opened my mouth, I was ready with my plan, my course of action seemed clear, and all the voices in my head were in agreement. But what came out of my mouth was, "I want my Valentino couture black-lace midheel peep-toe pumps back. The ones I had to sacrifice to you last week in order to get you to appear."

CHAPTER
FORTY

The devil's eyebrows arched. "I see."

I didn't say anything else. I couldn't; it felt like my vocal cords had fused together. I wanted to take it back. I would never take it back. I had to take it back. I couldn't take it back. I'd given up a friend for shoes, and I had no idea how to fix it.

Another long moment went by. Laura had a deer-in-the-headlights look, if the deer was about to be run over by a convoy of semis. Garrett was still waiting patiently. His (misguided) faith in me was touching; he must assume I had some sort of sinister plan. And I did. My plan was, essentially, *Oh shit!* The Ant was still on the fence, trying to figure out the best direction to jump.

Satan said, "You have no idea how much pain this admission is costing me: I underestimated you. So yes, you may have your property back. They're in your closet as we speak, between the Tory Burch suede clogs and the Franco Sarto animal-print clogs."

Way to rub it in, Lady of Lies. Clogs! Clogs are the new stiletto! Should have asked for Christian Louboutin to exist in this timeline.

"And as a . . . as a token of future goodwill, Antonia is also waiting for you."

Don't say anything. Don't say anything. FOR THE LOVE OF GOD, DO NOT SAY ANYTHING FOR AT LEAST TEN SECONDS.

"I trust there won't be anything else at this time?"

Three-Mississippi-four-Mississippi-five-Mississippi . . .

"I—that's—" Laura clearly thought I was having one of my . . . what had she and Garrett called it? A my-brain-isn't-here look. She must have figured that since the chances were good I was daydreaming about a shoe sale, she'd better fill in the conversation gap. "That's very kind, Mother."

"It certainly is," Satan agreed.

. . . six-Mississippi-seven-Mississippi-eight-Mississippi . . .

That was as long as I could hold out. "Antonia will be waiting for us? This isn't a monkey's paw deal, is it?" My voice was heavy with suspicion. "She's not a zombie with maggots in her hair and a mouth full of dirt, is she?"

"Only if she's taken up some alarming new hobbies."

I couldn't believe it. I couldn't *believe* it. I broke Satan's neck and she gave me presents? No smiting? No scourging? No locusts or whatever Satan visited upon people?

Shit! Not that I minded a locust-free visit. Locust-free visits were always good. But this was a sobering thought. Make that a terrifying thought.

It was all true. It was all going to happen. I was going to turn into someone so awful, the devil paled by comparison. Someone so awful, the devil had to stay on her good side. And I didn't know how to fix it or even slow the process.

I wasn't unaware of the irony, either. I hated, hated, *hated* when Sinclair kept things from me, but lately I'd been keeping a few secrets of my own. Irony, you are a vicious bitch.

Meanwhile, Satan had incorrectly interpreted (thank goodness) my silence.

"The book isn't mine to give or to take," she said as if in response to what she thought I was thinking. There was thinly veiled irritation in her voice. Single-ply toilet paper thin. "If that's what you're working your way up to asking about. That's up to my daughter; it's always been up to her."

Uh. It has? News to *this* girl.

I was getting the hang of this, maybe. I just looked at her.

"The Book of the Dead isn't mine to give back," Satan said, making a sound like she'd been holding her breath.

Like she wasn't sure what I would say and was *holding her breath* while she waited to find out. Which wasn't possible. Maybe in the future I'd be a badass tyrannical jerk with no color sense and zombies for footmen (ewww!), but right now I was just a woman in despair because Christian's parents never met. A woman who'd broken the devil's neck on impulse. "This was all Laura's idea. It's for her to decide whether or not to give it back to you."

"Reeeeally." I gave Laura a sideways glance. This was believable and I was sure the Lady of Lies was making a bold departure by telling the truth. Laura certainly looked like a dog who knew she'd piddled on the good rug. "Then I guess we'll talk about that some other time."

"There's no need to raise your voice."

I had raised my voice? I was pretty sure I hadn't. I was positive I hadn't. It was no secret from me when I raised my voice, what with the shrieky tenor and adrenaline surge. And . . . was the devil *nervous*? Stop me if you've heard this before: what kind of weird-ass timeline *was* this?

Aw, nuts. Lucifer was still talking. "You should thank her."

"Yeah, hold your breath waiting for *that* to happen."

"That's not necessary, Mother, Betsy doesn't owe me anything."

"She was—"

"So maybe we should go?" Laura asked, looking at me

with eyes so wide the whites were showing all around, like a scared horse. She'd interrupted. She'd interrupted one of her elders! Unthinkable. The timeline was going mad. "We should go."

"Betsy for certain, but you may remain if you like, Laura." Satan looked right at me. "You should thank her because she was just trying to protect you."

"Aw. That's sweet, Satan. And I definitely need advice from you on when and where to trot out good manners."

"She didn't want you to know—"

"Mother." Laura's voice, sharp and heavy with warning.

"—what you'll do—"

"Mother!"

"—to Eric Sinclair in the future and—"

"Stop it!"

"—believe me, it's far worse than anything that happened to him before."

I stared at them all: mother, daughter, stepmother. "What is she talking about?"

"Nothing!"

"Everything," Satan said, so softly it was almost a whisper. A whisper I could feel at the base of my spine.

"It's not set in stone, Betsy, and it's not as bad as you think it—"

"It's not set in stone, Laura's right, she's always right

because she's so quaintly honest." The devil tittered, clearly amused at the thought of an Antichrist who tried never to lie. "It's set in *flesh*. That's what the book *is*."

"Why are you doing this?" Laura managed to force through gritted teeth. They were almost nose-to-nose. Their wings stirred and fluttered in their agitation. "Why are you doing this right now?"

Laura winced as soon as the question was out of her mouth, and I could see Lucifer had grabbed her. All four fingers and the thumb were deeply sunk into Laura's arm. "Because I. Don't. Lose."

"I don't like this, I don't like any of this, all of you just stop, ohpleasedon'tfight," the Ant moaned. We ignored her.

"What's she talking about, little sister?" I'd never been so angry and so afraid in my life . . . and that included getting run down in the road like a squirrel. "What in the book is about Sinclair?" This . . . it all made sense. This was why Satan would only give me the ability to read it after I helped Laura with her powers. And why Laura took it and wouldn't let me see it. The book predicted something terrible (like death, again) happening to the king of the vampires! "Out with it, Laura. I've already strangled one pain in my ass today."

Satan laughed harder. She had, I was sorry to say, a great laugh, a throaty chuckle-y laugh. "The book isn't *about* Sinclair. It *is* Sinclair!"

I blinked. I understood the words, but they didn't make sense in context. The book was Sinclair, like, what? They were one and the same? What the heck was that supposed to—

"My, I can almost smell your cortex burning as you labor to puzzle this out. Literally, the book is Eric Sinclair. It's *his* skin the book is written on."

Ouch. Nice try, Satan, but this girl wasn't biting. Finally, finally I was wising up to the devil. She was humiliated because I'd bounced her off the walls of her own office, and it didn't take her long to figure out the best and most vicious place to hit me was the center of my heart. Where I kept Sinclair, of course.

"Nice try," I said. "If I knew you a little less, I'd have fallen for it. Now. We really should head out, but don't think this hasn't been fun, although it hasn't, and don't think we haven't enjoyed your company, although we haven't." I looked at Laura and Garrett. "You guys ready to go?"

"Yes. Go. Yes." Satan made a visible effort to stop laughing. "This way it's even better. Oh, I never thought of this! Much, *much* better. Go with my blessing."

"Yeah, because if there's one thing I don't like to travel without, it's the devil's blessing."

Instead of getting pissy, she was getting more and more cheerful. Weird. Would Thorazine work on Satan? "Away,

Vampire Queen. And never, ever forget: I warned you, and your response was insolence."

"Yeah, thanks, it was fun strangling you, let's never, ever do lunch." I looked at Laura, who was playing Statues all by herself. "Uh, Laura? You want to unclench and make us a doorway already?"

She looked at Satan, then at me. She blinked, licked her lips, and tried a smile. It looked all right if you didn't mind sharks. The poor kid . . . she couldn't even make her expressions lie. It was so cute! She really hated confrontations (unless she was killing someone; then she overcame her shyness). I couldn't imagine how difficult this had been for her. It's hard, I think, for anyone to stand up to their mother, even mothers that weren't fallen angels. Laura did great. I was proud to be with her . . . so proud she was my sister.

"Yes, we've . . . we've worn out your welcome," she managed. I squashed the urge to put my arm around her. For one thing, her wings were still out and I had no idea how to encircle her shoulders without getting a faceful of feathers. For another, I didn't want Satan to see that as weakness, on either of our parts. "So we'll go. We'll go right now."

"That would imply you'd *been* welcomed," the Ant said, rallying. Guess she'd finally figured out which way to jump, because she went back to her desk and sat behind it. "Next time, call before you come."

"I don't have hell's phone number."

"Precisely," the Ant said. Ouch! She got me! That dead bitch got me.

It was all right. We'd gotten what we came for, and then some. I felt like doing a victory dance.

Things were going to work out.

They really were.

Laura carved a hole in the universe and the three of us stepped through it. I realized something that both impressed and scared me: Laura didn't have to smack me anymore to tap into her powers. When just a few days ago, she had to practically beat me with a two by four just to drop through a doorway to end up somewhere she couldn't plan for.

I noticed we were exactly where I wanted to go: my bedroom in the mansion.

Laura was catching on fast. Scary-fast. I was so glad she was on our side.

"Well! That was stressful and weird and probably illegal, or at least immoral. It was like a family reunion where nobody can find the booze. Also, you are really getting the hang of this teleporting-around-the-time-stream thing."

"I'd better be." Laura sounded unaccustomedly grim. The confrontation, of course. We'd been to hell and back (several times) and lived to tell the tale. I'd be worried if she didn't sound grim. "We're going to need everything, we're going to have to learn and master everything, just to tread water. And we're already behind."

"I know, I know." I didn't, actually. Behind what? Learn everything to tread water? Sure, whatever, your doctor told you not to mix your medications, right? She picked the oddest times to be grim and determined. Didn't she know? It was over. If this were a book, it'd be the end. If it were a movie, we'd be showing the hilarious outtakes while the audience surged toward the restrooms.

"Dammit, Betsy—"

"I'm not taking this lightly!" I added, raising my hands like I was a liquor-store clerk and she was a crack-addled petty thief. It was never a good sign when the Antichrist dropped expletives. "Just let me enjoy the moment, okay? You've agreed to give back the book, the devil's pissed at us, and—"

"Hey!"

"—and Antonia—"

"Dammit, what the hell?"

I looked—*that* was a familiar voice. And it was coming from my closet. "And Antonia—the good one—oh my God, I can't believe it . . . I mean, I believe it, but it's so unreal! Even though it's happening so, by definition, it's very real."

"I didn't exactly agree to give—" Laura began.

Muffled, from the far back corner of my walk-in: "Somebody better tell me what the hell I'm doing in this closet *right now*!"

"And Antonia's back," I finished. I'd recognize those growled dulcet tones anywhere.

"Betsy, about the book . . . we're going to need it, and I'm going to help you, and I think together we can fix things, but I didn't agree to—"

"Whoa!" I scrambled out of the way as Garrett darted down the hallway toward my room. Only my vampire nimbleness saved me from getting squished when he flew across the threshold. He didn't so much open my closet door as yank it off its hinges. Then Antonia was rushing out—clogs flew everywhere—and into his arms so quickly she knocked him over. They practically made their own shock wave when they came together: *ka-WHAM!*

Momentum brought them sliding to a stop about a foot from my ankles. I could see Antonia looked exactly as she had in life . . . still beautiful (it was disgusting how many werewolves and vamps were stupidly gorgeous). She had the build of a swimsuit model and the complexion of an Irish milkmaid who put sunscreen on before she even got out of bed. Soooo irritating. And hell must have a terrific salon, because her lustrous dark hair shone and her lean limbs were as finely toned as ever. In fact, I could see more of her limbs than I wanted as the two of them were ripping off each other's clothes.

Wait. They issued clothing in hell? Or did you have to, I don't know, pack a suitcase? Or a steamer trunk?

While I pondered this fascinating quandary, Antonia looked up long enough from trying to devour Garrett alive—that's how it looked to me, anyway—to say, "Hey, bimbo. Thanks for the ticket out of hell."

For Antonia, that was sincere, heartfelt, tearful gratitude. Heck, *I* was almost tearing up at the warmth of her thanks. I covered it pretty well, though. "Don't have sex with him in here, you whore."

Predictably, they both ignored me. "Hey. Hey! You can pay me back by fixing the closet door you broke through. And by doing that somewhere else. Oh, come on! Do not, do *not* have sex on my bedroom floor. At least move the extra shoes out of the . . . oh, God. Oh my *God*. How did you do that? I can't even imagine how you did that to something as big as—"

Laura had seized my elbow and was dragging me away

from the scene of desecration. Thank goodness, because although I didn't want them to defile my carpet, I wanted to see them do it even less. Yet I was frozen. The whole thing was like a shuttle crash in slow motion. You know how in action movies the hero always leaps forward in slow motion to stop something terrible? And you can hear his long, drawn-out, "Noooooooooo . . . !" Yeah. It was exactly like that, except I didn't have to pay $8.75 to see it.

"At least move my end table—" The crash of shattering glass cut me off. "You guys! Gross! I forbid it! I'm the queen of the vampires and you can't have sex right now on my . . . oh, man. That's not gonna come out." I looked at Laura as she mercifully pulled my bedroom door shut. "That won't ever come out, Laura. And there isn't a dry cleaner on the planet who will touch it. See? See what I have to deal with?"

Laura was unmoved by their romantic reunion and my revulsion at what I had (almost) seen. "We should go tell your husband everything that's happened."

"Okay. Do we have a CliffsNotes version? Because telling Sinclair every single detail will take a long time. Hey, let's start with me making your mom my bitch and finish with 'and now Garrett and Antonia are defiling our bedroom with fluids no one should be able to voluntarily produce much less spread around.' And can we leave out the part where I meant to ask for Antonia but asked for footgear instead?"

"Under no circumstances do we tell him every single detail."

I nodded, relieved. "Oh, great. We're on the same page, then."

"Not quite. But maybe soon. Listen . . ."

I listened. But the Antichrist seemed to have trouble finding words. She just looked at me and shook her head, but I didn't understand why. Head-shake: I'm a little overwhelmed? Head-shake: I can't believe what Garrett did with your bedspread? Head-shake: I'm scared what my mom will do next?

"We have a lot to do."

"Okay. No, wait. That sucks. And you're wrong. If this was a book, this would be the part at the end where we're all relieved that things worked out and everybody's happy. The end. Cue cheesy montage music, probably something sad by Stevie Nicks."

"No."

"Kenny Loggins?"

"What?"

"Come on, we just got back. From *hell* (again), if you're not keeping score. That's worth celebrating. That's worth resting on our laurels for at least a week, right?"

Laura was shaking her head so much, for a moment I worried she was having a seizure. "Betsy, I don't mean to tell you your business, except I think it's maybe my business, too, and I'm not sure what just happened is what you think just happened. Because—"

"Are you serious? Were you not just inside the hellhole formerly known as my bedroom? What just happened— what is, ugh, *still* happening is exactly what I thought was happening. Sinclair isn't going to take this well. Maybe we should go check in to the Marriott for a while . . . until the fumigators come at the least . . ."

"Betsy, please shut up! You have no idea how serious things are!"

"You're right. And *you* don't know when it's time to relax and lighten up. It's not your fault—it's your upbringing. Your folks are so busy helping their fellow man they never stop and smell the fabric softener. This is the part—"

"This isn't a book, Betsy. It's your life. It's all our lives."

I ignored the buzzkilling wench. "—where we do fun things for ourselves while telling everyone about our zany adventures. Then, as in every episode of *South Park*, we talk about what we've learned. Then we rest up for a few days or weeks or (let's hope!) months, and then something weird and terrible happens that we have to drop everything and fix. And that terrible thing sort of takes over our lives for a few days, and then we figure out how to fix the problem, and the whole celebration cycle starts all over again."

"We have a *lot* to do," she said again. "A lot to get ready for." Laura sounded grim and resolute, which was pretty cool. I felt frazzled and freaked, which was pretty normal. I was glad Antonia was back, glad Garrett had his girlfriend back, glad I'd kicked the devil's ass, glad Laura had sided with me at a crucial time, glad we weren't fighting anymore.

But everything had happened so quickly! Shoot, two weeks ago I had never been to hell, to the past, to the future. Two weeks ago, Garrett and Antonia were dead and my mom was living the single life in Hastings. Two weeks ago, Christian Louboutin was getting ready for the rollout of his spring . . .

But that was too painful to think about.

"Maybe I'll sow salt in my bedroom when those two are done. That seems to be the safest thing to do. That's not an overreaction, right?"

"Yes, do that." Laura sounded distracted, but she never wavered in her determination to haul me away from the scene of the (ongoing) crime. "Listen, we need to find Sinclair. And we need to talk to the Marc Thing."

"Oh . . . shit!"

I'd forgotten. I'd completely forgotten. We had unfinished business, triumph in hell or no triumph.

The laurel-resting would have to wait, dammit.

CHAPTER
FORTY-TWO

We rushed into the basement. Our dank, gross, creepy, you've-seen-this-in-every-horror-movie basement. There had been corpses down there, good guys and bad guys, and don't get me started on the tunnel system. Yeah. *Tunnel system.* I'd told Sinclair I felt like I was in a *Roadrunner* cartoon, but sometimes it was more like an episode of *Scooby Doo.* "And I would have gotten away with stealing the Book of the Dead if it wasn't for you meddling kids."

The basement stretched the length and width of the house, which was amazing any way you looked at it. The mansion, as the word implies, was not small.

We charged down the stairs, down a couple of hallways, past the kitchen (I could see someone in there but we were in too much of a hurry to slow down), down more stairs, and then we were in the gloom and stink of our ancient, dank, yucky basement.

I figured they must have been keeping him in one of the old wine cellars. Yeah, "one of," implying we had more than one, and we did. But I could honestly say I didn't know all that much about it . . . I disliked the basement almost as much as I disliked the attic (nothing good ever comes from the attic!). I was able to count on one hand the number of times I'd ventured down there, and that was the way I hoped to keep it.

Anyway, the wine cellars were solidly built, cool (but not damp or chilly), and best of all, they had enormous heavy wooden doors with old-fashioned bolts. Bolts! Like it was a medieval dungeon! Three of them (two more than anyone ever needed for anything, *ever*), each as thick as my wrist. What the previous owners needed bolts on the outside for I didn't know and didn't want to know.

It was a pretty good place to keep an insane, and insanely strong, vampire. Even if he wriggled or tore through eight rolls of duct tape, he had the bolts (three!) to contend with. It likely wouldn't keep him forever, but long enough for someone to realize what the Marc Thing was up to and cough up the old standby: "Look out! He's getting away!"

And I knew he was. I *knew* it. We hadn't come far enough

into the basement to see the wine cellar door, but I knew it would be hanging half off its hinges. I knew the door would be smashed and battered, and maybe a friend or relative lying nearby, unconscious or dead, and when we ventured into the room itself, we'd see splinters of chair and shreds of duct tape. We'd stare at each other in dismay and wonder how we could have been so stupid.

It would be like every movie that ever had a villain trussed in a corner ("Nobody puts Villain in the corner."), except that unlike poor unsuspecting fictional characters, *I* should have known better. The villain would wait until there was sufficient distraction (like the heroine roaring off to see her mom and then falling abruptly out of touch with the home base because she ran into a streetlight and then went to hell), then escape just long enough to fuck things up all the way around. Then, recapture. Then defeat. But all too late to undo whatever it was the bad guy did while he was unfettered.

So, as we rushed around a corner, I already knew what to expect, was already pissed at myself for being such a movie cliché dumbass.

In fact, I was *so* sure of what we'd find, I ran into the closed and bolted door so hard I gave myself a nosebleed and actually grayed out for a minute.

It took a long, long time to fall down. Long enough for

me to think about what a pleasant surprise it was, about
how the movies didn't necessarily get everything right, that
I should have had more faith in my roommates, that . . .

. . . that . . .

(Ow.)

CHAPTER FORTY-THREE

". . . be all right?"

". . . her a minute."

". . . right into the door, I couldn't—"

". . . bleeding stopped."

". . . anything I can do."

Jumble. Jumble of soft, soft words in my soft, soft head. Getting clearer, though. Oh, goody. I was going to live. I just wasn't going to live it *down.*

"No one is blaming you, Laura." My husband's voice. And that was his hand, holding mine. "I'm going to carry her up to our bedroom, and—"

"No! God, no!" My eyes flew open. "Please. Please don't go in there, and don't take me in there. You don't know,

Sinclair. You just don't." I looked around the small circle of faces. Tina, N/Dick, Jessica, Laura. "None of you can understand the true horror of what's happening in our room right now."

"You'd better be concussed at the very least," my best friend informed me. "Do you know how many stairs I gotta climb to get out of this shithole?"

"And Sinclair was wrong," I told my sister. "I'm blaming you. Why didn't you stop me?"

"How could I? You were like the bionic woman down here. I barely saw the door was locked before you smacked straight into it."

"Well, I . . . I thought we would find something else." I felt something wet on my lip and wiped the back of my hand across my mouth. My entire face ached. My hand came away trickling my sluggish undead blood. "Dammit. Tell me I didn't break my nose."

"You seem fine," Sinclair soothed.

"Ha! If you've got a medical degree, Sink Lair, it's the first I'm hearing about it." I started to sit up, ignoring the many helping hands. It's not that I wasn't grateful. Okay, I wasn't grateful. But I was more embarrassed than anything else. So intent on rescue I ran smack into a closed door and knocked myself out . . . not *too* lame. "Where's Marc? Shouldn't he be trying to take my nonexistent pulse?"

"In there." Tina pointed to the closed, bolted door.

"Not that Marc. The one that's alive, sane, and not (too) creepy."

"In there."

I blinked, then realized what she'd said. "What? You've locked him in there with the Marc Thing? What, did he lose the coin toss?"

"No, it's—"

"What the hell is the matter with all of you?" Sheesh. I go back to hell for a couple of hours and everyone back home checked their IQ at the door.

I was on my feet in a flash, fumbling with the bolts and then yanking them aside to open the door. Instead of helping, they just stood around and watched me. Unbelievable! I heaved it open (sucker was heavy) and made ready to dash into the room to save Marc from the profound idiocy of my room—

Both Marcs, who had been in deep discussion, looked up at me.

"What?" they said in unison.

I stared. I had to; it was an interesting sight to say the least. I saw in an instant why my roommates hadn't been concerned: the Marc Thing was still trussed, and though our Marc had been locked in with him, he was festooned with crosses.

Yep. Crosses were hanging everywhere off our Marc . . . if he so much as shifted his weight, the Marc Thing flinched back and couldn't look at him. And the duct tape was holding up beautifully.

The perfect interrogation technique. I was stunned at the simple brilliance of it. Because who would the Marc Thing be most likely to talk to? His younger self, of course. And who'd be the best judge of whether his old dead self was prevaricating or covering up? His younger self, of course.

"Ohhhh."

"Uh-huh," Jessica said, smug.

"Hey." Our Marc waved casually. "You're back, finally."

"Yeah, well, I've been busy."

"So we hear." Sinclair had taken out a handkerchief (who still carried those?) and was tenderly wiping the blood off my face. "Besting the devil and freeing our friend's soul."

"I'm not sure how the soul/body thing works in hell," I confessed. "Think about it . . . Antonia's body was buried on Cape Cod. But now her body is back here, alive. It's not her soul. She's flesh and blood again." Gah, didn't I know it. Mustn't . . . think . . . about bedroom . . . carnage . . . "I mean, how does that even work?"

Laura blinked. "Huh. I didn't even think about that, Betsy. That *is* weird."

"I have so much to tell you." I realized I'd been leaning

on Sinclair since I'd climbed to my feet. "And, um, I'm sorry I didn't tell you about going back to hell."

"No. You are not."

"Okay, well, I'm sorry I—"

"You are not."

"Okay, okay, but look how great it turned out!"

"That," my husband said, "is why you didn't wake up on the bottom of the Mississippi River."

"Please." I flapped a hand at him. "Like you'd ever hurt me."

He sighed. He looked grim, but then leaned forward, pulled me into his arms, and rubbed his chin on the top of my head. I guess I was supposed to find that loving and comforting, but all it did was mash my sore nose. "No, but I can dream."

"I gotta get going," our Marc said, standing. He backed out of the wine cell (I had decided the wine cellar needed a new name), which was smart. Dozens of crosses were pointed at the Marc Thing the whole time it took our Marc to cross to the doorway. He'd agreed to be locked in with it, but protected himself with tons of jewelry. Meanwhile, even if the Marc Thing *did* do something stupid, he still had the (three) bolts to get through. "I'll see you guys later."

"Don't be a stranger!" the Marc Thing called with eerie, and inappropriate, cheer. Hearing that raspy cold voice sounding high and enthusiastic made me feel a little like throwing up. Or throwing myself at another locked cellar/

cell door. "Send me lots and lots and lots and lots of post-cards! I love getting mail!"

Marc pushed past me and I let him. He'd had a look on his face I didn't like, but understood. He looked sort of . . . it was hard to describe . . . unplugged? Sort of vaguely uneasy but also thoughtful . . . like he'd been given tons of info and was having trouble making sense of it.

That was probably exactly what he was going through.

We watched him climb the stairs like an old man. When he was out of sight, I said, "It can be pretty terrible, finding out about terrible things that you haven't even done yet which will make the future terrible. I'll go talk to him."

"Give him a few minutes," Sinclair advised.

"Yeah, you're right. The Marc Thing probably blew his mind."

"That is it *exactly*," the Thing agreed. "We caught up on current events . . . I can't grow hair in new and gorgeous ways anymore, but perhaps a wig? Perhaps . . . a Justin Bieber?"

"Perhaps gross," I suggested.

"Is Antonia really back from hell? It's not that I thought Laura was lying. It just seems . . . it's incredible."

"She's here," the Marc Thing said, "but she's not here. Antonia's dead. You just can't help yourself, can you? You pretend you hate change, but it's what you constantly bring us to."

"Pull the other one, Fang. Tina, you haven't even heard the whole story yet!" And wouldn't for a while, since Laura and I were in full agreement that the gang didn't need every single dull detail. I'd hit her with the highlights, emphasizing how cool and awesome I'd been in hell.

"Then lead on." Sinclair courteously gestured to the stairs, bowing slightly at the waist. The bow did nothing to hide his amused grin. "And regale us, my own."

So that's what I did. That's what kills me, that's the part I couldn't stop thinking about after. When I could bear to think about any of it at all.

I *did*.

CHAPTER
FORTY-FOUR

Half an hour later, we were back in smoothie central. I was just getting to the (abbreviated) part where Satan asked me what she'd have to do to get me to leave hell (I'd been there, and I could still hardly believe it) when Garrett and Antonia walked in.

"I don't even want to ask. Did you at least set our room on fire as you were leaving? Fire purifies everything," I said as an aside to Sinclair, who was staring at Antonia. "I'm pretty sure."

"My God!" Jessica said, pointing. Normally she tried not to bust the first commandment when friendly vampires were around, but I think in this case, her shock was justified.

"My God!" Antonia said, pointing at Jessica's belly.

"I know," I said, nodding. "Shocking and disgusting, isn't it?"

"You're just so gigantic." Antonia seemed hypnotized. I knew exactly how she felt. "How . . . how do you even *move*? What are you eating? Who are you eating?"

"Great to have you back," Jessica said dryly. "The place just wasn't the same without you. You can take that any way you want."

Tina had crossed the room and, to my surprise, gave Antonia a spontaneous hug. It's not that they were enemies in the old days, it was just that spontaneous affectionate gestures from the coolly controlled Tina were unusual. "I'm looking right at you and I can't believe my eyes." She looked at me and I was a little uncomfortable at the unmistakable admiration in her face. "And you *did* this? This is amazing. I am . . . amazed." She shook her head. "Just . . . it's just very, very amazing."

"Hey, a deal's a deal." Vain jerk that I was, even I could get a bit uncomfortable with what looked like borderline hero-worship. Maybe not even borderline. "I promised Garrett I'd try to get Antonia back, and here she is."

"No," Garrett said. They had both gotten dressed—and in their own clothes. That was interesting. That meant Garrett had never packed any of Antonia's things away.

"Hey, don't underestimate yourself. Antonia, he was right

there with Laura and me the whole time. Wasn't he, Laura? You know the saying 'I'd follow you to hell and back'? Garrett really did!" Have I mentioned I *loved* this timeline's Garrett? Quiet, but cool under pressure, and utterly reliable.

Laura had been quietly sipping her smoothie and not contributing much to the conversation. This was cool by me, since I was definitely the hero of this story and was happy to explain that to anyone who wanted to listen. It had been a long few days. I didn't blame her for being drained, poor kid.

"No," Garrett said again. He'd brought his knitting bag into the kitchen and was having Antonia help him roll yarn. Which I never understood at all. The yarn comes in a nice wrapped-up little package . . . which the knitter then unwraps. Then rewraps into a ball. Dumb. I could feel myself slipping into a boredom-induced coma just thinking about it. "You didn't promise."

"Uh-huh, sure, anyway, then the devil was all 'hey, bitch, you can't do that to me in my own waiting room' and I was all 'so call a cop, jerk' and—wait. What?"

"You didn't."

Now we were all looking at him in surprise, even Antonia.

"It's not what you did, it's what I did," Garrett said, idly rolling eggplant purple yarn into an eggplant purple ball. "When Betsy came back—when she didn't remember Jessica being pregnant and didn't remember I was alive, I lied. She doesn't want to think she's a bad person, so she helped. But she didn't." He looked at me for a half second, a casual glance before pausing to root around in his knitting bag. "She didn't promise."

If he'd blown up, we couldn't have been more shocked. Garrett saying more than a sentence or two at a time was hard to wrap our minds around. To think that quickly . . . come up with a plan . . . execute the plan . . . and lie? It was almost unthinkable.

"I . . . I . . . I . . ." *I hate the new Garrett!* I sat there staring like a goldfish. "I have no idea how to react to this."

(Privately. React privately. You and I will discuss this later, my own. At length.) Sinclair's voice in my head was grim and cool, but he kept a pleasant expression on his face as he watched Garrett. Sometimes I loved this telepathy stuff.

(I don't know what . . . you know what? I don't even know what to think about this, never mind what to do.)

(Privately. At length.)

I casually picked up my smoothie and nodded. Damn right, privately at length. I didn't mind being tricked . . . okay, that wasn't true, I *did* mind. I mind that Garrett could lie, and do it so well no one questioned his word.

"Hey, Marc hasn't come back down yet. You know he's gonna make me play back all the gossip for him if he misses it."

"I think he's trying to grab some shut-eye . . . he volunteered to pull a double tonight."

"You want to—" I got up and grabbed an empty glass from the dish strainer, held it out to Jessica, and she carefully filled it with our new flavor experiment, blueberry-banana-and-more-blueberries. Sinclair was such a freak for strawberries, we were glad to have some variety. "I'll run this up to him. If he's snoozing, I can just throw it back in the freezer."

"Tell him he can have the Mystery Machine for the weekend. He met somebody," she said to the group. "He wants to head up to Superior for a couple of days."

"Good for him," I said, pleased. Marc's social life usually sucked rocks. I was glad he'd put himself out there again. Let me say for the zillionth time: how had he not found some great guy and settled down with a white picket fence to raise beagle puppies and pick fights with Superior Court rulings on gay marriage? That sounded like a pretty great happily-ever-after to me.

And Marc deserved it more than most. I always understood why he'd become a doctor . . . it was hard to imagine him doing anything else. Or being anything else. It was a cliché, but he was a giver. He was never happier than when a situation was improved (hysterical roommates with boy trouble, hysterical fourth grader with a scalp laceration, hysterical vampire queen in a Louboutin-less timeline) by his presence.

It didn't take long to get to his room—he was a floor above Sinclair and me, in a little-used section of the mansion. He had taken the smallest bedroom for himself, not for the size, but the view . . . when the leaves were gone, you could see the Mississippi from his window.

I rapped on his closed door. He wasn't blasting the Eurythmics, so he was probably awake. He said nothing soothed him to sleep faster than Annie Lennox's throaty, raspy, penetrating voice. It takes all kinds of people to make a world, or so my mother says.

"Marc?" I rapped harder. "I come bearing smoothies and gossip."

Nothing.

Nothing at all.

And I started to get a bad feeling. It wasn't any one thing, it was *all* of them. Marc, spending who-knew-how-long with the Marc Thing. Not coming to the kitchen, but going up into his room, alone. No music blasting . . . but no one answering when he knocked. Any one of these things would be slightly odd. Add them together and . . . there it was! My bad feeling.

I tried the knob, already knowing it would be locked. And it was, of course. I'd seen *this* movie, too. And it was no problem for me; I raised my foot and slammed my heel into the wood just below the lock. The old, thin door didn't have a chance. It didn't have a chance because who worried about locked bedroom doors? Not us! That was who! No, we just worried about big, heavy, securely bolted doors in the basement, doors behind which we thought Marc was interrogating the Marc Thing. Doors behind which we thought the Marc Thing would tell us important things to fear in the future.

I was betting that was exactly what he had done.

I shoved the rest of the door open with a twist of my hip as I shot inside. The room was small, like I mentioned, and I immediately saw what he had done.

I saw what he had snuck off to do when no one would come looking for him, when no one would notice he was missing, when no one would stop telling stories about how great she was, when no one would call 911, when no one would stop him from killing himself, when no one would drown out the Marc Thing's voice urging, commanding, informing, ordering.

No one. Not even me? How about, especially not me.

CHAPTER
FORTY-FIVE

The Artist Formerly Known as Nick had taken care of everything. He had been incredible. Commanding and calm, he made the right calls and talked to the right people. He and Sinclair had a private conversation. Then he talked to us in a comforting way and we were glad he was there to help us, we were glad he was our friend, he did everything right, he made it all easier.

He did everything except bring Marc back to life, and if he could have done that, he would have.

I had held Jessica while she wept. Pulled her away from his doorway (my screams, I'm sorry to say, brought everyone on the run) so she wouldn't hear him being zipped into the body bag, so she wouldn't see him get loaded into the ambulance like a sack of grain.

When she was cried out, I tucked her in the way her own mother never had. I calmly waited until she fell asleep. I left her room.

Nick had left with the ambulance. Laura had left also . . . I didn't notice when. That was a problem. Her rapid comings and goings, her scary-fast grasp of teleportation . . . I would have to deal with that, and soon.

Not right now, though. Right now I had something else to deal with.

Sinclair and Tina were in the kitchen speaking in low voices. They stopped when they saw me.

"Are you—" Sinclair cut himself off when he saw my expression. "Very stupid question, I apologize. Nick went to the hospital."

"I know."

"Jessica is asleep?"

"Yeah."

"Laura?"

"Gone. I don't know when." And I didn't know where. The future? The past? The Mall of America? No idea. "I'll worry about that later."

I picked up a kitchen chair and set it upside down on the

table we all shared, except Marc because Marc was dead; Marc killed himself and he'd never share this table again, except he would.

Yes.

I snapped off one of the chair legs. Turned. Marched toward the basement. Went into the basement. Walked the length of the basement until I came to the securely bolted door. Marc, after he'd been programmed or mojo'd into killing himself, had still thought of our safety. Had locked everything nice and tight before heading upstairs to inject himself with a lethal amount of opiates.

He was beautiful in death. It was true what people said. Sometimes people really do look like they're only sleeping. Marc had taken care to leave a gorgeous corpse. This was good, because I wasn't going to let him stay dead for long.

Oh, and the letter. He left that behind, too. But I wasn't letting *anybody* see that. Not for a while, at least.

It seemed to take a long, long time to reach the wine cell. Tina and Sinclair had silently followed me. When I got there and shot the first of the bolts, they both automatically stepped forward to help me.

"No."

"What?" Tina was startled out of her usual deference. I think my tone surprised her.

"No. I'm doing this. Me. By myself. You two are not

invited. I'm opening this door and going in. Then you'll close it and lock it. When I knock, open it back up and let me out."

Sinclair looked as distressed as I'd seen him. "Elizabeth, do not be silly, we can't—"

"I'm not *asking*, Sinclair. Don't make the mistake of thinking this is a discussion. Now. Unless you want a shit day to turn apocalyptic, do what I tell you."

They did what I told them.

Good thing, too.

CHAPTER
FORTY-SIX

"Oh, you're here!" The Marc Thing was very pleased, if the futile wriggling against the tape was an indication. "Finally! Ready to kill me?"

"Yes."

"Oh, goody, goody, goody! I've been waiting soooo—" He cut himself off and peered at me. "You aren't being a meanie, are you? You're not teasing? You'll do it?"

"I'm not being a meanie. I'll absolutely kill you."

"Hooray!"

"I just want to know why." I crossed the room so I could get a better look at his face. His eyes. "Why did you come? Was it just to talk yourself into killing yourself? Was it so Ancient Me wouldn't get her hooks into you?"

"You want to know why." He seemed to ponder this for a moment, then brightened. He looked a little like his old self, and those moments, they were actually the worst. When I could see the man he had been. God, he was damaged, so damaged. But yeah, the worst was when he almost looked like my Marc. When he looked like my friend. "Because you don't know why! Right? You don't! I'm here so I won't be here and you don't know!"

I squatted in front of him. Any other time I'd be yanking on my hair trying to puzzle this out, but I was frozen inside right now. Dead, almost. I felt like I could outwait anything, even the ravings of a crazy dead guy. "Right. I don't know. So tell me. I bet the devil fixed it so you could follow us back. Maybe you were supposed to kill me, too? Or as many of us as you could?

"See, it occurred to me that we didn't have to stay in hell more than a few minutes. It occurred to me that maybe Satan was stalling. To give you time to work on Marc. To give you time to set up his suicide. And maybe my murder?"

"Your murder? Who'd murder you?"

"You want a list?"

"You couldn't murder you, so you didn't murder you."

Patience was one thing, but this was starting to make me want to find a razor and trim his ears right off his skull.

"Can you try to tell me in a way that isn't completely crazy? If it's at all possible?"

"The devil won't ever kill you. And her daughter won't, either. They can't. But you can kill you. It was you, Betsy-Wetsy."

"You mean it was my fault because in hell I—"

He whipped his head back and forth so fast his features were a frightening blur for half a second. It was such an unnatural way for a human body to move, it was shocking to watch. I almost fell backward onto the chilly cement. Then he seemed to catch hold of himself.

"You did it. You sent me back, Betsy."

I was glad I hadn't fallen, because I wouldn't have been able to get up after hearing that. "Ancient Me sent you back?"

"She didn't remember and she asked and when I didn't remember she sent me back. You did things and said things. In the future. You did things and the other you, the old you, the bad bad you, she didn't remember those things happening. She saw a chance to save him. Them," he added, like that would clarify the babble. "She sent me back to save me. Because if she didn't let all those bad things happen to me, then bad things wouldn't happen to her."

I was trying to follow this. I had a vague memory of a sort of shoving match in Ancient Betsy's office. Her surprise . . . her shock, even. So when Laura and I left, she thought about it. And talked to the Marc Thing about it. And sent him back to kill/save my Marc.

Because if I didn't make Marc into the Marc Thing, maybe there were other awful, awful things I wouldn't do.

Maybe such an insanely risky maneuver was all she *could* do. Maybe she decided it was worth the risk if it meant she might keep her soul. By saving the world from . . . well . . . *her* . . . she was also saving her family and friends.

I could almost see her, the older me, sitting at her icky big old desk and wondering: will I feel it when the time stream shifts? Or will I never notice it at all? Will I still be . . . me? Or will I be her? Or someone else, someone like neither one of us?

I didn't know. That was the maddening part. I knew quite a bit now about the future, but only enough for despair. Not near enough for hope.

"I saved me," the Marc Thing said, so softly and pleasantly he sounded a lot like the guy who'd killed himself upstairs two hours ago. "Now you have to save you." He nodded at the chair leg stake in my hand. I hadn't bothered to hide it. What would have been the point?

"She never," he said. I realized he was crying a little. "She could never finish me. She couldn't save me and then she couldn't end it for me, so I went on and on and on and got more and more and more dead and she knew that killing me would have been killing the last smallest scrap of her humanity and she wouldn't. She couldn't. And I loved her and I hated her, but mostly I loved her because she was *her* and if you kill me you won't ever be her. And Marc will never be me."

I was staring at the floor. I couldn't look at him. It was definitely the worst when he sounded almost human. "I'm sorry that happened to you."

"*Happened* to me?" He laughed. "You're making it sound like I was in an earthquake. You're sorry *you did that* to me. Right?"

"Right."

"I know. That's why I know you can kill me. Right? If *you* kill me, you'll have all kinds of scraps of humanity left. Tons of scraps! Only I don't want to see it coming. I never could stand to even get a shot if I knew when the needle was going to hit . . . isn't that the dumbest thing you've ever heard?"

"No."

"It's why I was going to jump. The night we met, remember? I was going to jump and die, but you caught me before I fell. You caught me before I even jumped. And kept catching me and catching me and because you were so used to saving me you could never let me go. You will now, though, right?"

"Yes."

"I liked being a doctor," he said wistfully. "I think if I hadn't been murdered I would have been happy doing that for the—"

I stood. Looked closely . . . yes. The Marc Thing was gone. A chair leg slammed through the chest and out the back of the chair he was trussed to would do that every time.

I'd saved him, and maybe myself.

And he hadn't seen it coming.

CHAPTER FORTY-SEVEN

"I'm sorry about how I was in the basement. It's your vampire kingdom, too. I just really wanted to take care of it myself."

"I was not offended, my queen, only worried." We were in the wreck of our bedroom . . . seeing all the shattered evidence of Garrett and Antonia's reunion was the first thing that made me smile in hours. "Also, I cannot live like this."

"We're outta here." I zipped closed the bag I'd been packing. "I don't want to see this place for a couple of days. Jessica's already called contractors. I told her we'd be at the downtown Marriott." And Jessica would tell the others. And we'd all take a couple of days to recover from our shattered sense of How Things Should Be. And then we'd sit at the smoothie table and try not to notice how Marc wasn't there.

And then we would make a plan. And then we would save the day.

Which would be tricky, given everyone's new identities. The timeline wasn't the only thing that had changed.

Garrett, who barely opened his mouth to ask for a new skein of yarn, or whatever they called the units of measurement yarn came in, had learned to lie. Satan, who practically invented lying, had taken to sprinkling some truth in with her usual doses of fibs. Laura, who almost never lied, was learning to leave out important chunks of stories. And I, *I'd* learned that if I could keep my damned mouth shut once in a while, people would do things or tell me things they hadn't planned on.

Because, although I was thrilled Antonia (the good one) was alive and back with us, I would never forget that I hadn't asked for her. I'd asked for something else . . . something that didn't have a soul and a pulse. Instead of asking for the life of a friend, I'd asked for a thing that couldn't love me back. And that meant . . .

That meant I was not the hero of the story. In fact, it was looking more and more like Laura was the hero.

So what did that make me?

Exactly.

"I was so happy when we got back from hell. I felt like I'd fixed everything, how fucking dumb could I be?" I was telling this to Sinclair's chest, because he'd folded me back into his arms. Luckily my nose had healed.

"Shhh, do not do this to yourself."

"If not me, then who?" I thought that was a better-than-fair question. Who was gonna call the vampire queen on her shit, when even the vampire king deferred to her if she was bitchy enough?

Exactly.

"It will seem so strange here without Marc," Sinclair mused. "And even stranger to have Antonia back. Once I thought I had seen so much, life could teach me no more. How fucking dumb could *that* be?"

I had to laugh; I knew how he felt. And he had a good point about Antonia.

Was it always going to be like this? Would I have to give up something wonderful to get something wonderful back? Because I did not sign on for this shit.

No. Because I knew things I hadn't known before this awful, awful hooray-Thanksgiving-will-soon-be-here, *awful* month of November.

I knew dead didn't mean dead.

I knew you could come back. Or the devil could *give* you back.

Oh, and one more thing. The devil badly, badly needed to stay on my good side.

"Marc's dead, but he won't be for long," I vowed, shaking in Sinclair's arms. From anguish or fright or rage, I couldn't tell. Maybe it was all three, a new emotion, one so novel to me I couldn't identify it. "I'm gonna get Marc back. He didn't leave a gorgeous corpse behind for no reason . . . he knows I'll get him back."

"Elizabeth—"

"I'll get him back, Sinclair, no matter what I have to do. And no matter who gets in my way."

"I believe you, my queen, and will help you any way I can."

"Yes, I know. We'll get him back and then we'll all have smoothies and laugh about how worried we were the day he died."

And the devil help anyone who got in my way. It would *have* to be the devil.

God, it was clear, was on *my* side.

Dear Betsy,

I'm gone now, but not forever. Couldn't leave without giving you the scoop, though, so listen up.

First, although you will, don't blame yourself. Even as I'm writing this I get that it's a waste of time, but I'm jumping in and trying anyway. Again: don't blame yourself, dumbass.

I wanted to do this. Frankly, I have inclinations like this all the time. It even runs in my family (along with alcoholism and the ability to make hospital corners). Shit, remember the night we met? I was about to do a swan dive off the hospital roof and you wouldn't let me. You saved me . . . for a while.

Now I'm saving you.

It's only fair.

It's also only fair to tell you that you shouldn't blame the others, either. In hindsight, letting me spend time alone talking with the dead me seems careless and risky, right? Sure . . . in hindsight.

But it's not their fault. I only told them the stuff they'd find most helpful, the bare minimum. The stuff that would make them feel okay about me going back into that room. And back. And back. They're as invested in saving you as I am. And they don't know a fifth of what I know.

Listening to yourself tell yourself about the awful things you'll do someday is an experience, I won't deny it. But before you break off a chair leg or something and march into the basement to kill the other me like John Wayne with fangs, please believe that the other Marc DID NOT MOJO ME INTO DOING THIS.

He just told me what would happen to me if I didn't. Believe me, it was not a difficult choice. At all. And hey, I'm a man comfortable with opiates. When I went, honey, I went wrecked.

So I've saved myself. And I've saved you. And I was glad of the chance. Do you know why?

Because I love you, dumbass. From the moment we met. You've been like the little sister I never wanted. (That's a joke.

Not a very good one, I agree.) And right now you're thinking dark thoughts about how you can't protect your friends and being the vamp queen has ruined your life and no job in the world is worth this and how could you not see what I was going to do, blah-blah-blah, why me, I want shoes, this is hard, I hate everything, more shoes, blah-blah-blah.

But here's the thing, and it's the stone truth: knowing you has only ever made me feel one way. Not scared, not horny, not crazed, not pissed, not despairing, not thwarted. Lucky.

Knowing you has made me feel lucky. Even now, prepping this little opiate cocktail, I feel lucky. I'm controlling how I leave this world, something that poor bastard down in the basement couldn't do. And look at the price he paid!

By doing this to myself, I'm undoing some seriously bad shit.

But don't take my word for it.

Go to the basement, and ask me. Ask me for yourself. You won't like what I say, but you'll see the truth behind his awful smile.

I love you.

I will see you again. Believe it.

Your friend,
Marc

Appendix

I've never written an appendix before! Which I guess I find exciting, what with the exclamation point and all. In fact, I still have my original appendix. No appendectomy for this girl. But enough about the operations I haven't had . . . the reason I've put this here at the end is because several readers asked for the complete Civil War ABCs Betsy memorized when she was four. Which I found flattering, yet weird. So here it is.

BETSY'S ABCS

A is for Antietam

B is for Buchanan (James)

C is for Confederate States of America

D is for Davis (Jefferson)

Appendix

E is for Emancipation Proclamation

F is for Fort Sumter

G is for Gettysburg

H is for Harriet Beecher Stowe

I is for Indian Territory (Oklahoma Civil War)

J is for Jackson (Andrew)

K is for King Cotton

L is for Lincoln (Abraham)

M is for Mason-Dixon Line

N is for Navy (Confederate, Union)

O is for O'Neal (Rose)

P is for Pickens (Francis W.)

Q is for Quinine

R is for Reconstruction

S is for Sherman (William Tecumseh)

T is for Thomas (George H.)

U is for *Uncle Tom's Cabin*

Appendix

V is for Vicksburg

W is for War Between the States

X is for XXV Corps

Y is for Yankee

Z is for Zebulon Baird Vance

And now, a sneak preview of

Undead and Unstable

*the eleventh installment of
the Betsy the Vampire Queen series
by MaryJanice Davidson,
available soon from Berkley Sensation*

"What are you talking about, she's dead?"

"Betsy, I've got a zillion things to do, what with creating life and all, so could you pay attention when I talk? Did you not see my lips moving?"

They're always moving, I thought but did not say. Jessica was too cold except when she was too hot, and she was starving except when she was throwing up or, worse, starving *while* throwing up. (I didn't even want to think how that was possible.) She was angry and she was joyful. She was tearful and she was enraged. She was pissed and she was venomous. She was pissed except when she was crying and—God please help us all—crying-pissed was the worst. The very worst. My super vamp powers were no match for crying-pissed.

Wrong again, I realized, remembering what I'd overheard last night from two floors away. When Jessica wasn't eating or pissed or nesting or pissed or nagging, she was horny. Sometimes eating olives stuffed with garlic made her horny. Worst yet: she was often all those things at once, nesting and horny and pissed and horny and hungry and horny. Nobody was brave enough to touch the olive jar in the kitchen. And poor Detective Nick/Dick was starting to shamble about the place with the nine-hundred-yard stare.

"Well, look." I was afraid to. Look at what? At her? Why? Maybe she was wearing her giant yellow and blue circus-tent shirt in a terrifying attempt to seduce me. The thought made me want to simultaneously burst into gales of laughter and throw up in my mouth. "She is."

I peeked, prepared for the worst. Pre-pregnancy Jess had nothing in the knockers department, but that was no longer the case. Luckily, seduction wasn't on her mind right now.

We stared down at the body with more than a little surprise. "What happened?"

"No idea. I was headed to the basement and I almost tripped over the body." Jessica patted her gigantic belly. Like the stairway wasn't dusty and dark and claustrophobic enough without the Fetus of the Darned hogging her stomach, and also most of the stairwell. "I could have broken my neck! Do you know what a fall could have done to me at this stage of my pregnancy?"

Nothing. Nothing at all. The Michelin Man had less padding. I didn't say anything, though. I wasn't ever going to be lauded for my genius, but that didn't mean I was an *utter* dumbass.

This is going to sound terrible (even for me), but you know that series *Game of Thrones*? I guess the show did so well that now there are books about the *Game of Thrones*. Or maybe the books came first—I dunno. I quit reading fantasy before I was of voting age. There was just too much of "I shall draw the mystical sword of Eldenwurst, thus named Soulsucker, and with mine eldritch blade will smite all enemies of the fey. But fear not, all ye who tremble before Soulsucker, I shall rule with a just hand and also the Council of Geeks, now ye and ye, bring me fifty virgins and lots of mead." Those books lose me right around chapter two. Anyway, I'd never read the books, but the show was pretty cool, and I got hooked on it.

No. That wasn't true. Marc had a huge crush on the Khal Drogo character, and *he* got me hooked on it. So he'd come off shift from the ER and we'd raid the DVR and rhapsodize about Drogo's unbelievable shoulders and what a doucheboat Viserys was.

Wow, getting ahead of myself more than usual . . . Okay,

so, in the first season of *Game of Thrones*, the unborn baby of one of the main characters was called the Stallion Who Mounted the World, a scary yet cool nickname. Jessica was sporting the Belly That Ate the World.

"I'm glad you didn't trip." I sighed and glanced back down at the dead cat. "She's looked better." An understatement. Giselle didn't look like she was sleeping; dead bodies never looked like they were sleeping.

And Giselle, the cat who'd gotten me into this whole vampire queen mess in the first place, was most definitely not sleeping. Her eyes were cloudy slits. Her mouth was frozen, half open, and she was thin, but not dangerously so . . . She'd always been scrawny. And she was old . . . I'd had her for more than ten years. She just showed up one day and refused to leave, so I got into the habit of feeding and sheltering her. I guess that's how babies and roommates show up, too. You feed 'em and they just never leave.

For ten years we each pretended the other didn't exist. Our only interactions were during mealtimes. (Hers. Not mine.) And since I'd moved us into the mansion way back when, plenty of other people were happy to take over the chore. The mansion was so big, my pet (except I'd never really had that warm connection to her, and you couldn't say I was her pet: see above, lack of connection) and I would go for days without seeing each other, which suited us both.

I'd been killed the first time trying to coax Giselle into coming out of bad weather. I wasn't paying attention during the snowstorm while I coaxed, and got creamed by a Pontiac Aztec. Giselle, natch, scampered off without a scratch. She was the only thing in my life that found my resurrection boring.

Now here I was, looking down at her skinny dead body and realizing I had one more task to finish before I could consider all my pet responsibilities fulfilled.

"Ugh."

"Yeah."

"Are there shovels in the shed?"

"Several."

"There are? Really?" What terrible news; I couldn't pull the old "I can't do this unpleasant chore even though I really want to because we don't have the right equipment" ploy. Another wonderful day in a shit week. Month, come to think of it!

Giselle, you insensitive jerk, you couldn't have done this a month ago? Or a month later? You gotta do it now, while fate and/or karma is really piling it on, and Jessica wouldn't have pedis without me, and we'd burned out the motor on one of the smoothie blenders? Typical cat: not one thought for how her death would inconvenience me. Andrew Vachss, the best noir-y writer in the history of the genre, called cats the lap dancers of the animal world. Give them attention, and they're there. Stop, and they're outta there.

Well, she was outta here, all right.

"Next time," I announced, "I'm getting a dog."

Jessica snorted. She knew that was a lie. She knew why it was a lie, too, but was too nice to call me on it just then. "If memory serves, you didn't exactly *get* Giselle."

"Your memory serves." I bent and gingerly picked up the body, then held it at arm's length like a luau platter. "Yuck."

"Oh, will you suck it up? You've seen how many hideously mangled dead vampires, never mind mangled regular people (who were bad, but still mangled), and friends have been shot in front of you and/or killed themselves in your house, but you're squicking out over a cat? *That* cat? Hey, I just said suck to a vampire." Weirdly, that seemed to please her. "That's all you've been doing lately, complaining about how awful it is to be white and pretty and rich and married to the hottest guy in the state of Minnesota. Okay, Marc *did* kill himself," she admitted. "*That* you can bitch about."

I gave her a look, but decided not to shove her down the stairs. *She's creating life, she's creating life. Oh, and she stuck with me when I came back from the dead. Also: creating life.* "Can you go grab me an old sheet or pillowcase or something?"

"Sure." My hugely pregnant pal was looking right at me, her brown eyes thoughtful. Since she was a couple steps above, I started to get scared. If she tripped, she'd kill us both. "Sorry about this, Betsy. And sorry about a couple seconds ago. My back feels like someone's resting a set of barbells on it, and the barbells are on fire. It's not doing much for my mood. And, you know . . ." She let out such a gusty sigh, I wondered if she'd float off the stairs like Mary Poppins. "The random deaths and stuff."

I waved it away, all of it, along with my fears of being squashed to death by a pregnant woman while clutching the dead body of my cat and fretting over my lack of pedicures. "Par for the corpse. Whoa. At least that didn't come off as a Freudian slip or anything." Had I said that? Had I *really*?

She giggled, thank God, then turned and started climbing the stairs again. Non-pregnant Jessica was rail-thin and favored nail polish in colors like Day Glo Orange or Aged Chartreuse (which, in case you're wondering, looks like vomit dried on a nail bed). Pregnant Jessica was not rail-thin. At all. Quite the opposite of rail-thin. What would that be, bovine fat? And she was avoiding all the chemicals she could. *All* of 'em! Which was only impossible.

So among other things, she wouldn't go near a salon (or sushi, of all things . . . like eighty zillion Japanese women didn't eat sushi when they were knocked up?), which was a personal disaster for me. She was using all-natural deodorant (the kind that didn't work), natural hair product (the kind that makes her look like a pissed-off Rastafarian), and when I gently suggested a fetal-friendly salon massage, she slammed the door in my face (so to speak). All of this to say: this sucks. Who goes to a salon alone? Big-time boring. If Marc were still here, he'd love—

Never mind.

I followed her up the stairs, lugging my dead cat. If I was smarter, or nicer, I'd think something like, *It's sad that the cat keeled over, but Jessica's baby will be born soon and out of death comes life, a full circle of life, hakuna matata and suchlike.*

But I'm not smart, or nice, so what I thought was: *And the hits, they keep on coming. Nobody ever considers my feelings when they decide to keel over and die on the basement stairs. And the second I'm confronted with an evil poopie diaper, I'm going to go right out of my teeny tiny mind.*

Still, if our situations were reversed, I'd want Giselle to bury me. Wait. I absolutely wouldn't, since half the time I had no idea if I was dead-for-real or could wake up screaming on an autopsy table or, worse, sleep through Macy's annual shoe sale, so I wouldn't trust a cat to know, either. Shit, *coroners* sometimes couldn't tell. I actually knew that for a fact; it was a horrible thing to know for a fact. At least two certified medical examiners hadn't been able to tell if I was dead.

Besides, our situations weren't reversed. And I could

whine and bitch until the sun rose and set and rose again, and it'd still be my responsibility.

So after Jessica got me a yellowed pillowcase, I stuffed Giselle into it and out I went, into the deep November cold, searching for some meaning in all the crazy shit that had been happening since Giselle got me killed a few years ago. And I was also searching for a shovel. And after this yucko errand, I would be searching for a booze smoothie.

Ah, the glamorous life of a vampire queen.

All sheds smell the same. Even though I hadn't been in all sheds, I was confident in making that claim. Dirt and paint, and grass cuttings and mouse poop. Once out in the getting-deep-in-a-hurry twilight typical of late fall in Minnesota, I circled around to the backyard and into the shed, then set my bag-o'-cat on the dirt floor to begin poking around.

The shed was as creaky and old as the mansion, which had been built in 1860 or 1720 or 1410 or something like that. And I figured the last time the shed had been cleaned was while Lincoln was still walking around on the planet.

Also, like all sheds, it was magical in that once you got inside the thing, it seemed much much bigger. *It's like a ballroom in here!* A filthy ballroom that smelled like mouse poop and had a dirt floor. I couldn't tell if this chore was more annoying due to enhanced vampiric senses, or because I was an indifferent homeowner. There was probably another reason it was annoying, too . . . Right! My cat was dead.

I found a shovel-sized piece of rust, grabbed the pillow-case, and went to the far backyard. Though I had zero interest in doing my chores, I couldn't fault the mansion for it's size and beauty, and I liked that the yard was huge, not one of the postage-stamp ones . . . a good trick in a city the size of St. Paul.

I walked toward a couple of the big old oak trees in the left corner . . . they were naked now, but in the summer and fall they were pretty great. If Giselle had ever expressed a desire to be buried (by me), I liked to think she'd have asked for this corner.

It had been a mild fall, and there were only a couple of inches of snow on the ground, but the dirt beneath was frozen. Normally it'd be a bitch to dig, but I had confidence in my weird undead strength. There were a few upsides to being the queen of all vampires.

(I was almost getting to the point where I could think of myself with that title and not go into gales of amazed laughter. Give me another seventy or eighty years, and I might be able to pull it off with my puh-puh-puh-poker face.)

Me being me, I tended to focus more on the downside. *Stupid strength of the damned* was on the list along with *stupid super hearing* and *stupid keen sense of smell*. Also me being me, the downside list was much, much longer. And as the shovel slid through frozen dirt like a smoothie blade through a raspberry, another downside came to me. One I'd stupidly discounted when I took on my duties as the undertaker of the dead cat who'd gotten me killed and then inconveniently died on our stairs. The dogs. They were a *huuuuge* downside.

And here they came, thundering toward me in a slobbering charge.

Betsy's back again as a vampire queen who finds herself an unlucky (but fashionable) passenger on the road to damnation . . .

From *New York Times* bestselling author
MaryJanice Davidson

UNDEAD *AND* UNSTABLE

Betsy's had a rough go of it lately, what with her friend Marc's death and her sister Laura's new job offer—to replace Satan down under. All Laura has to do is kill Betsy, her own flesh and blood.

Now Betsy and Marc—who's not *quite* dead yet—have a war to win, one that gives sibling rivalry a whole new name . . .

Praise for the Undead series

"Delightful, wicked fun!"
—Christine Feehan, #1 *New York Times* bestselling author

"Think *Sex and the City* . . .
filled with demons and vampires."
—*Publishers Weekly*

facebook.com/maryjanicedavidson
maryjanicedavidson.net
facebook.com/ProjectParanormalBooks
penguin.com

M1023T1211

Vampire Queen Betsy Taylor returns in the ninth
novel in the *New York Times* bestselling series from

MaryJanice Davidson

Undead and Unfinished

Vampire Queen Betsy Taylor is having a tough time
getting through the Book of the Dead—until the
Devil strikes a bargain. She offers Betsy a chance to
finish the cursed (literally!) thing and finally discover
all its mysteries. There's just one catch . . .

Betsy and her half sister, Laura, have to go to Hell
long enough for Laura to embrace her dark heritage
(after a rebellious youth of charity work) and finally
make nice with her mother, aka Lucifer. That means
interacting with their family's past. In doing so,
they're impacting the future in ways they never anticipated. Of course, that's what Mother wanted all
along. Damn her.

M614T1209